Rush Revere

and the

FIRST PATRIOTS

*Time-Travel Adventures with
Exceptional Americans*

RUSH
LIMBAUGH

THRESHOLD EDITIONS

NEW YORK   LONDON   TORONTO   SYDNEY   NEW DELHI

Threshold Editions
A Division of Simon & Schuster, Inc.
1230 Avenue of the Americas
New York, NY 10020

First Threshold Editions hardcover edition March 2014

THRESHOLD EDITIONS and colophon are trademarks of Simon & Schuster, Inc.

For information about special discounts for bulk purchases,
please contact Simon & Schuster Special Sales at
1-866-506-1949 or business@simonandschuster.com.

The Simon & Schuster Speakers Bureau can bring authors to your live event.
For more information or to book an event contact the Simon & Schuster Speakers
Bureau at 1-866-248-3049 or visit our website at www.simonspeakers.com.

Interior design by Ruth Lee-Mui
Jacket design by Ariana Dingman
Jacket painting by Christopher Hiers

Manufactured in the United States of America

1   3   5   7   9   10   8   6   4   2

Library of Congress Cataloging-in-Publication Data

Limbaugh, Rush H.
Rush Revere and the first patriots / Rush Limbaugh.
pages   cm
1. Boston (Mass.)—History—Revolution, 1775–1783—Juvenile fiction.
[1. Boston (Mass.)—History—Revolution, 1775–1783—Fiction.   2. United
States—History—Revolution, 1775–1783—Fiction.   3. Teachers—
Fiction.   4. Time travel—Fiction.   5. Middle schools—Fiction.
6. Schools—Fiction.]   I. Title.
PZ7.L6352Ruw   2014
[Fic]—dc23   2013049742
ISBN 978-1-4767-5588-5
ISBN 978-1-4767-5592-2 (ebook)

*To my audience, the genuine people who
make this country work.*

*In honor of our friend Vince Flynn,
"Keep The Faith!"*

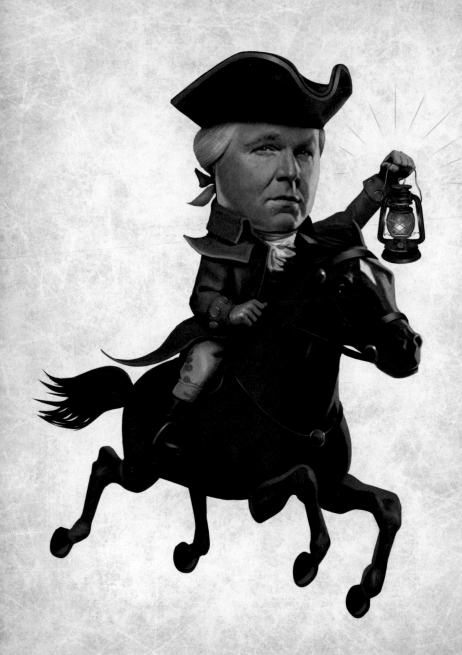

Foreword

I have dedicated this book to some people I often talk about, people for whom I have the greatest respect and admiration. These are the everyday, anonymous people we don't know by name, who are out there working hard, trying their best to play by the rules and do what is right. They are not trying to become famous, because they don't have time. They are focused on things they consider far more important than fame and notoriety. These people define the uniquely American spirit. They are the people who, I like to say, "make America work."

These people truly define and exemplify what is great about this country. Their toil and productivity created an abundance of goods, services, and compassion the likes of which the world had never before seen. Because of them, the Unites States of America became a beacon of hope and inspiration for people all over the world. Americans are some of the most generous, dedicated, courageous, and sincere people in the world. More often than not, the moment a tragedy or natural disaster happens in a small hometown or anywhere in the world, Americans sprint to help "thy neighbor" not only because they can but because they choose to.

The Pilgrims planted the seeds of all of this. After they arrived in what became Plymouth Colony on the *Mayflower* in 1620, under the leadership of William Bradford, they not only survived in the very tough conditions, they thrived. The Pilgrims and Native Americans shared tips of survival. The colonies grew rapidly in size and population. Small towns developed with streets, stores, hospitals, and libraries.

The Pilgrims paved the way for future Patriots to bond together and stand up for their beliefs. Many everyday people, people who were not famous at the time, took grave risks to voice their opinion, especially when counter to mainstream thought. From the early days of the Pilgrims onward, the people of the original colonies wanted to be free: free to believe in God and practice their religion, free to provide and care for their own families and futures, free to own their own property, and free to speak out against those who wanted to control their lives. We are all the descendants of the people who held these first American ideals.

If it hadn't been for these everyday people, people who faced difficult circumstances and overcame what seemed like overwhelming odds, transforming themselves into the leaders of their time, our country would not be the wonderful place it is today. We should never lose sight of this. These leaders took chances—great risks—and thought far beyond their own lives for the greater good of others.

This is the American spirit that we share with our ancestors.

Children across the country have been writing in to me, talking about reading *Rush Revere and the Brave Pilgrims*. Parents, grandparents, stepparents, and siblings from Honolulu to Bangor are sharing the message about true American history:

a message that recognizes our failures and challenges, yes, but also one that does not focus on these failures and challenges alone! One that celebrates freedom and the American spirit!

I love America, and I want you—and everyone!—to also love America. It is my fervent hope that in learning the history of our country you will be inspired to learn about the people, traditions, and institutions that make this a great country so that you will someday make your own contributions to these ideals. And someday maybe you will become a leader yourself. I really want you to be among the millions of ordinary people who accomplish extraordinary things and make America work.

So now it is time to delve into a new adventure and learn about some other people who stood up and got involved in order to further their dreams. My good buddy Rush Revere and his hilarious pal Liberty are going to take you back in time to the mid-eighteenth century, where you will meet some of the first Patriots!

So hold on tight and here we go . . . let's *rush, rush, rush into history!*

Prologue

Smoke billowed from the center of the large rioting mob. The year was 1765 and I was walking along a busy street in Boston, Massachusetts. Large colonial buildings surrounded me on either side; most were two-story rusty-red brick buildings but some were taller, three or four stories. Many shops and businesses lined the street—a silversmith, a candle maker, a clock maker, a bakery, a furniture store. The shops seemed endless. The last time I was near this location was 1621, soon after the Pilgrims landed on the *Mayflower*. It had grown tremendously! I wish my good buddy William Bradford could be with me! When I last saw him at the first Thanksgiving, he told me he knew Plymouth Colony would develop into an incredible country we call America! He was right, of course!

As I thought back to my conversations with William, I completely lost track of where I was going! All of sudden I found myself approaching hundreds of men dressed in colonial clothing looking eager to pick a fight. They were yelling things that I couldn't really understand, but it didn't sound like they were very happy. I noticed the smoke I had seen earlier was still coming from the center of the crowd!

Liberty, my horse, spoke loudly enough to be heard over the shouts of the mob and said, "If that's a fire up there I don't think they're roasting marshmallows. It's too bad because I do love a good marshmallow, but only if it's slightly browned on the outside and gooey in the middle. I mean I know some people like to set their marshmallow on fire and then quickly blow out the flame, but then all you get is that charred and blackened outside crust that tastes like charcoal. Not that I've ever eaten charcoal but I . . ."

"Liberty!" I said. "I appreciate knowing how you like your marshmallow cooked, but we're on a top-secret historical mission, remember?"

"Oh, yes, got it, Captain," Liberty said as he started humming the theme song to *Mission: Impossible.*

"Liberty!" I said. "Shhh."

"I was just trying to set the mood," he replied.

"Let's see if we can squeeze our way through the crowd and find out what's burning," I said.

"Call me crazy but normally I don't like to walk toward fires! I mean, can't we just assume they aren't making s'mores and hightail it out of here?"

"What happened to 'Got it, Captain'?" I asked with a grin.

"Right, okay. I'm in. Luckily, I'm wearing my fireproof saddle. Not! But seriously, you won't hear a peep out of me unless I catch on fire!"

"That'll never happen," I said with a wink. "You're too *cool* to ever catch on fire!"

"Well, that's true." Liberty smiled.

As we made our way toward the smoke I heard a number of comments that were very revealing about the mob's mood and motivation.

"This should send a message to that bloody King George III," said a man who wore his hair in a ponytail.

"Yeah, he thinks he can tax us and take our money to pay for his debts and support his military in America. We didn't vote for that!" said another man who wore a white wig.

"That's right," said a third man. "No taxation without representation!"

I was leading Liberty by his halter as someone bumped into me from the side. He might have knocked me down if I hadn't been holding on to Liberty.

The man slurred his words when he asked me, "Are you in support of the King or against him?"

I was caught by surprise. I'd intended to only observe what was happening. I quickly came up with something on the fly and replied, "Oh, well, I'm against anyone or anything that tries to control the people and withhold their freedoms."

"How do I know you're not just saying that? Maybe you're in support of the King and his Stamp Act and you're just saying you're not so we don't beat you to a pulp!"

I quickly realized that maybe Liberty was right! Maybe we shouldn't have walked toward the smoke, but my inquisitive mind just had to know!

"Who can vouch for ya?! Maybe you're really a spy!" shouted another man.

I felt several pairs of eyes glaring at me and realized I had no witnesses, no one who could vouch for my loyalty to the colonies and to this new America. The men stepped closer. It was obvious they weren't playing around. My palms started sweating and my heart was racing. I felt a nudge from my side. Liberty was trying to get my attention but I was frozen. He nudged me again with his nose, prodding me to hurry up with an answer. Hmm, think, Revere, think. Aha! Got it! Sure hope this works, I thought.

I finally said, "I do have someone who can vouch for me: my horse!"

The men surrounding me burst out laughing at the thought of it.

"Did you just say your horse can vouch for you!" said the man with the white wig.

It was clear that none of them believed me.

"Yes," I said with as much confidence as I could. "You see, I'm so passionate about America's freedoms that I've trained my horse, Liberty, to support the cause of freedom as well."

"You're going to have to do better than that," said the man with the ponytail, who got right in my face and grabbed my collar with both hands as if he was about to throw me.

"I will prove it," I said.

The man holding my collar released his grip and said, "You had better."

I straightened the collar on my coat and turned to look at Liberty. I asked, "Are we in support of King George?"

Liberty shook his head from side to side with big, sweeping strokes. When he finished he stuck out his tongue as if he were disgusted about something. My accusers thought this was very amusing as they all laughed out loud. Whew! I thought, wiping my sweaty palms on the sides of my pants.

I steadied my voice and said, "Are we against King George and the unfair taxes that he burdens us with?"

This time Liberty nodded and let out a high-pitched squeal that sounded like "heeeeeeeeee!"

I looked each of the men in the eye and said, "Do you know how long it takes to teach a horse verbal commands like that?" I wanted to say about ten seconds if he's a magical, time-traveling horse that can talk. Instead, I said, "It takes weeks and months, especially if the horse is stubborn and pigheaded!"

Liberty turned in my direction and gave me *the look*. The kind of look you give to someone when you think you might have just been insulted.

"Thankfully, I have a brilliant horse who can smell tyranny a mile away and who fights for freedom. In fact, this horse should be the mascot for the thirteen colonies! After all, his name is Liberty!" I said, proudly.

The performance seemed to work, as the three men slapped me on the back! "Good on ya! We'll see you later at the tavern. Only Patriots allowed."

"Sounds like a plan," I said, still nervous inside but trying to sound confident.

"Holy smokes!" I said, letting out a breath as they left.

"Go on, admit it, I came through for you, right?" Liberty teased. "I'm going to answer that for you. Liberty saves the day! Oh, and by the way, you didn't look nervous at all," he said with a heavy dose of sarcasm, "especially when that guy with a ponytail was about to put you in a headlock!" He laughed like it was the funniest thing he'd heard all week.

"Go ahead and laugh it up. The truth is, I was scared that they were going to use me as a punching bag!"

"I would never let that happen," Liberty said with a determined look. "You should always know that I've got your back, Rush Revere. Always! After all, we are best friends!"

I sighed with relief and smiled. "Thanks, Liberty," I said. "I owe you one, possibly even two."

"But you still want to know what's up with all the smoke? You know, we could just leave," Liberty prodded.

"Aren't you curious to know what's making all that smoke?" I asked.

"Not really," he said, sounding almost bored. "My nose only smells smoke, not food. Why start a fire if you're not going to cook something?"

Food was never far from Liberty's thoughts.

"Come on, let's continue our mission," I said.

We got close enough to see a bonfire blazing right in the middle of the street. We could hear the men shouting things like "Repeal the Stamp Act!" and "No more stamps!" Several members of the mob were throwing what looked like newspapers, books, and documents of all kinds. Even playing cards were being tossed in and consumed by the flames. And each item had a stamp on it.

"I know what this is," I said to Liberty. "The colonists are protesting the Stamp Act by throwing stamped documents onto the bonfire."

"I don't get it. What does the stamp have to do with anything?" asked Liberty.

"King George passed the Stamp Act without consulting the colonists. He basically decided that everyone in America who purchases anything made from paper should have to pay an extra charge for it—it's called a tax."

"No wonder they're ticked off. Didn't the colonists come to America to get away from the King's rule and be free from this kind of thing? It doesn't sound like the King really wants to let them go!" said Liberty.

Just then a voice shouted, "Redcoats! About two dozen with guns and bayonets are coming!"

I could see the glint of the bayonets. I could hear their boots against the pavement getting closer and closer. "Come on, Liberty! We better get out of here!"

I didn't have time to jump onto Liberty's saddle so I just sprinted as fast as I could. Liberty galloped ahead of me, looking back now and again to see if I was close behind.

"Now you want to run!? You could've listened to me when I said it was a bad idea to walk toward the fire, but nooooo," Liberty said.

Most of the mob dispersed from the scene as the fire was left unattended and burning in the street. We kept running until we were a safe distance away from the commotion. Finally, we slowed down to catch our breath.

As much as I wanted to stay to see what happened next, I knew it was time to hit the road, and fast! I said to Liberty, "Remind me to tell you more about the Stamp Act later."

"It's funny because whenever you say Stamp Act I think you're saying Stomp Act. You know, like stomping or clogging. Maybe I should put together a stomp act about the Stamp Act!"

"If you did I'm sure it would be something unforgettable! But first, let's get out of here before we run into British troops. Let's head over to that side street. I saw an alley earlier that should conceal us when we jump through the time portal."

I lifted myself up onto Liberty and we trotted over to the alley.

"Let's go!" I said as I gripped the horn on Liberty's saddle.

"Rush, rush, rushing from history," Liberty said as he started galloping toward the brick wall at the end of the alley. A swirling gold and purple hole started to open in front of the wall. Two more seconds and we jumped through the cosmic hole—our time portal to the twenty-first century. I was excited to get back to modern-day because tomorrow I had a very important appointment with the principal of Manchester Middle School!

Chapter 1

Hundreds of students wearing gold and black sweatshirts, hoodies, and jerseys swarmed the football stadium like honeybees in a hive. I guessed that the mascot of Manchester Middle School was a yellow jacket or hornet, but my suspicions were soon put to rest when I saw the actual mascot enter the field with a fluffy golden mane around a large catlike head. Obviously, Tommy, my favorite history student, played for the Manchester Lions. Whoever was inside the mascot costume was very acrobatic as the lion jumped up and did a perfect backflip. He or she stuck the landing and then pumped a large paw into the overcast sky as hundreds of students and families cheered with excitement.

I was glad to be back at Manchester Middle School and curious to know why the principal had asked to see me in his office after the game. You see, my horse and I had recently taught the Honors History class while the full-time teacher, Ms. Borrington, was on a leave of absence. I know what you're thinking. Did I just say I was teaching with a horse? Yes. Yes, I did. My horse, Liberty, is not just any horse. He's, well, special. He's sort of like the Lone Ranger's horse, Silver.

In fact, after I took Liberty to watch the Lone Ranger movie he said, "I should've tried out for the part of the Lone Ranger's horse, Silver. The part where Silver races across the top of those western buildings and then leaps onto that moving train was impressive. But that was clearly a stunt horse. Besides, if they had picked me I could've carried on an actual conversation with Tonto! Not to mention my superior good looks."

I didn't say he was humble, I said he was "special." Yes, Liberty can talk. Oh, and he can time-travel, too. What better way to teach history than actually going there. Jumping back in time is very cool!

I followed several students into the school stadium and started searching for Tommy. He had bright blond hair that was usually easy to spot. I was pretty sure he'd be at the game since he's the starting quarterback—a gifted athlete but a closet genius.

As I walked parallel to the sideline, looking up at the bleachers I heard a voice yell, "Mr. Revere, heads up!" I turned toward the green field and saw a distant player throw a football that was now spiraling directly toward me. The ball soared directly over a Lion who tried to intercept the ball but missed by just a few inches. Instinctively, my hands reached out and, surprisingly, I caught it. The Lion turned around and crouched in a defensive pose as if daring me to try to get past him. Then it motioned for me to come forward with its large mascot paws. I looked beyond the Lion at the player who threw the football. He waved and

I could see that he was smiling. Actually, he was laughing really hard! Wait a minute, that's Tommy!

Right then, I felt a hand pat me on the back. I turned and saw a familiar sweet face. "Freedom!" I said. She was another favorite student with some special gifts of her own. Her long, silky black hair had a purple feather clipped in it that complemented her tan skin and dark eyes. But it was her smile that was the most welcoming.

"Hi, Mr. Revere, it's great to see you again!" she said. "Looks like Tommy picked you!"

"What do you mean *picked me?*" I questioned.

"He picked you to challenge the Lion," she said, her smile even bigger than before. "It's a school tradition. Before every game the quarterback throws the football into the crowd. Typically, he picks someone who's walking along the sidelines. Whoever catches it gets to take on the Lion."

"And exactly what does *take on the Lion* mean?" I asked. By now it sounded like every person sitting in the bleachers was chanting *Run! Run! Run! Run!* Over and over, louder and louder, the crowd was clearly eager to see me in action, whatever that was. The Lion kept jumping up and down waving his large paws back and forth, encouraging the crowd to chant louder.

Freedom continued, "Oh, that means you have to try to get the ball past the Lion. If you do, then it's sort of considered a touchdown! It means good luck for our team if you score, and bad luck if the Lion sacks you."

"Sacks me?" I squeaked. "Here I thought I was only coming to the game to cheer on Tommy. Not be in the game."

"Oh, you can do it, Mr. Revere!" Freedom said, still smiling.

"Good luck!" She patted my shoulder and disappeared into the crowd.

"Come on! Run! Run! Run!" the crowd endlessly chanted.

Well, I decided it was time to show Manchester Middle School just what Rush Revere was made of. My Pilgrim hero William Bradford didn't doubt his goal of reaching the New World. He led the *Mayflower* ship from Europe to America, across the huge waves, water crashing on the deck of the boat. The Pilgrims learned to overcome their fear. They took every challenge head-on. They used their skills and their ingenuity to prosper and find success. If the Pilgrims could do that, I could figure out how to win this challenge and not be completely humiliated in front of the entire school!

I gripped the ball tighter against my side and started running. The crowd erupted with cheers as they saw me fearlessly take on the football feline. I moved a little to the left; the Lion moved with me. I moved a little to the right; the Lion adjusted again. When I was only five yards from my opponent I put the football behind my back and concealed it with both hands. It felt awkward running with a football behind my back, but it was all part of the plan. I slowed at four yards, a little slower at three yards. The Lion tilted his head, obviously confused as to why the ball was behind my back and why I was slowing. In that split second of confusion and with only two yards between us I bent forward ever so slightly and flipped the ball up and over my head. Before the Lion could react, the football soared above its shaggy head. I sprinted past the bewildered beast and turned to catch the ball as it drifted down. Pedaling backward, I reached out, caught the ball, and then landed on my backside. Immediately the crowd burst into cheers. Apparently, I had scored! I looked up and saw the Lion with his paws in front of its mascot face, shaking his head. Tommy ran up to me wearing his gold football helmet and said, "You did it! That was amazing! Nice job, Mr. Revere!"

"Whew!" I said as I stood up. "Thank you! A little positive thinking and hope for the best goes a long way!"

As Tommy and I walked to the sideline he said, "I'm really glad to see you! I kept hoping you'd come back to Manchester. Does this mean you're back to teach?"

"I'm not sure yet. Principal Sherman asked if I'd stop by after the game for a chat. He didn't say what it was about, but I knew I shouldn't miss it! I'm really glad he called or I wouldn't have known about the game. I was hoping you were playing today."

"I'm going to tell Principal Sherman that you have to come back!" Tommy said. "You're awesome! I mean you're the first substitute teacher that makes history remotely interesting or at all memorable!"

"I appreciate the compliment," I said, "but that might not be a good idea. If I remember correctly, Principal Sherman thinks you're always up to something. The troublemaker!" I smiled.

"That's a good point!" Tommy said with a laugh.

As we got to the sideline Tommy looked around and asked, "Hey, where's Liberty? I don't see him! Or smell him, for that matter!"

"No, Liberty has the day off," I said. "He's at a horse spa! A livery, remember?"

Tommy laughed. "That horse is so spoiled! A horse spa? As in massages and pedicures?"

"Ha, yes! That's what he calls it. He's actually just getting a bath but don't tell him that."

Freedom joined us from the bleachers. "Hi, Tommy," she said, seeming happy to see him. "Good job, Mr. Revere! I knew you would do it! You told us on the *Mayflower* not to doubt you and you were right!"

"Ha, I'm pretty sure I was talking about why the signing of the Mayflower Compact was a really important part of history, not about taking on the school mascot in front of a roaring crowd!" I said with a grin while brushing a grass stain off my knee.

Tommy chuckled and asked, "Hey, are you going to stay and watch the game?"

"Of course!" I said. "I sacrificed my body to get past your Lion and bring you good luck!" I winked at Freedom. "Speaking of good luck, that reminds me! Almost forgot!" I reached into my pocket and pulled out two musket balls given to me by Myles Standish, the military leader for the Pilgrims. "Do you remember when we all traveled back in time with Liberty to Plymouth Plantation in the year 1621?"

"How could we forget? That wasn't your average day at Manchester!" Freedom said.

"Quick pop quiz! Who was Myles Standish?" I asked.

Tommy laughed. "That's easy! He was the cool Pilgrim guy that taught me how to swordfight! He reminded me a lot of my friend's dad who was in the military and really strict. But Myles was still really nice. And he knew everything about fort building, which rocked!"

"Correct, Tommy, spot on! He was the military leader for the Pilgrims! Well, I brought something with me from Myles. I forgot I had them until Liberty and I got home." I held out my hand to show Tommy and Freedom the musket balls. They were as small as marbles but made of lead. They were round, smooth, and very shiny. "Myles told me that when the Indian Squanto stayed with the Pilgrims he taught them many things, like where to find the best striped bass, bluefish, and cod or how to catch eels or where to hunt for ducks and geese and deer."

"Wait! Did you say eels?" asked Tommy with his eyes wide.

"I did," I said, nodding. "Slimy, snakelike eels!"

"Awesome! I wish Squanto would've taught me how to hunt for eels!" said Tommy.

"You were probably busy swordfighting," Freedom teased. "Squanto taught me how to plant corn just like the Indians did back in the early, early, early colony days. And he gave me a special necklace."

I continued, "Let me finish my story. After coming back from fishing, Myles was gutting a big fish and inside he found these two musket balls."

"Really? The fish ate the lead balls? Wow, that fish must've been really hungry! I don't even think Liberty would eat lead balls!" said Tommy.

"Sure he would," I said, laughing, "if they were dipped in honey! Anyway, when Squanto heard the story he said that it was a sign of good fortune, a sign of good luck. He promised Myles that if he rubbed the musket balls between his fingers while making a wish, the good fortune from the balls would rub off and help him succeed in his next task!"

"And? Did it work?" Tommy asked with excitement.

I smiled and replied, "Myles rubbed the musket balls together each time he went hunting or fishing, and every time he had great success!"

"But that doesn't necessarily mean it was caused by—"

Freedom tried to say before I discreetly elbowed her in the shoulder as Tommy reached for the musket balls.

"I'm going to try it," Tommy said. He rubbed the balls between his fingers and said, "I want to have my best game today. No interceptions!" He handed me back the musket balls.

"Good luck, Tommy," I said.

"Yeah, good luck," said Freedom, smiling.

"Thanks, guys! Gotta go!" Tommy ran off toward his team.

Freedom and I headed back to the bleachers and found a place to sit. When the game ended, Tommy had completed four touchdown passes, a rushing touchdown, and zero interceptions! The Manchester Lions beat the Benedict Bulldogs 35–14. Call it luck or coincidence or whatever you like, but the fact is, Tommy had a super game! It's amazing what a positive mental attitude can do. Of course, a little bit of luck never hurts!

Soon thereafter, Freedom left with another friend and I decided to head over to the principal's office. As I was leaving the stadium I saw Tommy run over with his helmet off. His curly blond hair was matted to his head but his blue eyes were as lively as ever.

Tommy said, "Thanks for coming, Mr. Revere. It was great to see you. I think those musket balls must've worked! Tell Myles 'thanks' the next time you see him. By the way, have you gone back to see Plymouth Rock or visited your friend, William Bradford?"

"No, I haven't recently," I said. "I've really wanted to see how everything is progressing in the colonies, but I just haven't had the time."

"Are you working at the iced-tea company?" Tommy asked.

"Yes, and I've been helping a friend start a small business. I tell you, starting a business isn't easy! It takes a lot of long hours and hard work!" I said.

"Well, if you ever do time-jump to visit the first Pilgrims again, I want to go!" said Tommy. "I'd love to check in with all those guys, including Squanto! In fact, I made the coolest fort in my backyard with my new buddy, Cam. He just moved here from Colorado. I told him that I learned fort building from Myles Standish."

"And what did Cam say?" I asked curiously.

"He thought I was totally full of it! He said, 'Yeah right, and I bet you learned how to skateboard from Tony Hawk!'" Tommy said, imitating Cam.

"Do you blame him?" I asked, smiling. "Does Cam go to school here?"

"He just started. I'm trying to get him to try out for the football team. Hey, maybe you can get him into our Honors History class!" Tommy said.

I looked at my watch and realized I needed to hurry or I'd be late for my appointment with the principal.

"Well, it's great to see you, Tommy! You were a star out there today! I better get going and see what Principal Sherman wants."

"C'mon, Tommy!" yelled one of Tommy's teammates. Tommy waved goodbye to me and ran off while I headed into the school.

Although it was late in the day, there were still several students in the hallways. I saw Principal Sherman speaking to a couple of students near his office. I'd forgotten how he towered over everyone else. I'll admit that he made me a little intimidated. As I approached, the principal excused the students he was talking to and said, "Hello, Mr. Revere, thank you for taking the time to meet with me."

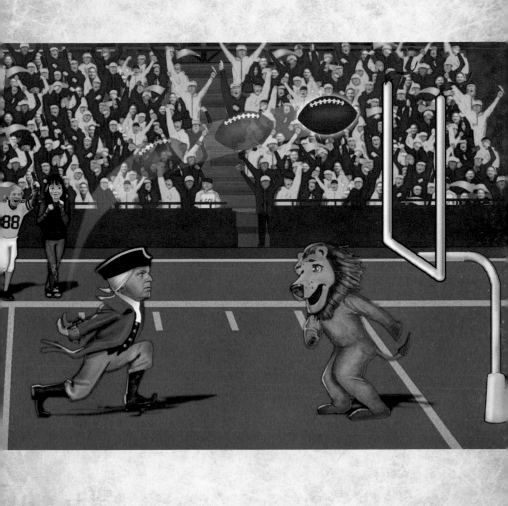

Principal Sherman was all business and got right to the point. He said, "Mrs. Borrington is going on vacation to the Caribbean to celebrate her wedding anniversary. Therefore, Manchester Middle School would like to invite you back to teach her class in the interim. We are low on substitute teachers and most of the kids seem to like your style."

"Thank you," I said. "History is my specialty and I think the students are wonderful."

"I say 'most of the kids' because there is one student that doesn't like you much."

"Oh, that's too bad," I said. Even though I was sure the disgruntled student was the principal's diva daughter, I asked, "What's the student's name?"

"Well, it's actually my daughter, Elizabeth. She strongly encouraged me to not have you return. However, I interviewed several other students who are enrolled in Honors History and they vouched for you as a competent teacher."

"I'm encouraged that the students feel this way and I'm happy to return to teach Honors History," I said. "And I do apologize that Elizabeth did not have the same experience that the other students shared. She's more than welcome to attend my class, if she would like to try it again." I decided it probably wasn't the best time to tell him that his daughter can be a bit of a brat!

"I'll see you tomorrow then, bright and early," said Principal Sherman as he excused himself.

I was excited about the chance to teach again. My first lesson covered the journey of the *Mayflower* from Europe to the New World! Personally, this had always been a favorite part of American history for me. It always amazed me that a group of 101 people would decide to set sail across the wide, scary ocean without really knowing where they were headed! It's not like they had an airline ticket and knew which airport they were landing at with a welcoming committee! They set out to find a new land of true freedom, where they could be themselves and improve their lives. I'm sure they couldn't have done it without strong leaders, like William Bradford, who rallied them together just when the journey was looking to be a lost cause! My mother used to do that on long car rides. Every time my brother and I thought we were going to go crazy waiting to stop for McDonald's, she would say, "Rusty, remember, it's mind over matter! Just think how much better that Happy Meal is going to taste knowing you went through long hours of pain and suffering to get it!" I always knew she was exaggerating! We weren't really suffering in the back of the car. The Pilgrims, however—they really struggled. They spent sixty-five brutal days with little food, cramped into a very tight space, in terribly hard conditions, with waves crashing all around them in the dark of night. I get a little seasick just thinking about it. Just like my mom, William Bradford encouraged the Pilgrims to keep their faith and trust that God would help them survive and prosper. When they finally landed in the New World, sadly many of the Pilgrims died that first winter due to the freezing temperatures, starvation, and disease. But William Bradford held their heads high, reminding them that they had set out on the journey to build a better life in a new place and that is exactly what they did!

William knew that the best way for each of the Pilgrim families to prosper in their new way of life was for each family to have a plot of land where they could build a home and work for themselves. Instead of putting all of their goods into a communal chest, William Bradford encouraged the Pilgrims to be on the same team, yet work hard to take care of their own families. He knew they would try their hardest if they knew they could keep the rewards of their hard work and labor. It's a lesson I've always tried to teach my own students. What if they all studied really hard for a test but no matter how hard they worked they would all get the same B grade as everyone else? Why would they ever try for an A?

Under William Bradford's leadership the Pilgrims quickly prospered. They befriended and traded with the Native Americans. Soon after, other ships like the *Mayflower* came to America after hearing the success that the Pilgrims were having. In only twenty years, that first colony, known as Plymouth Plantation, grew from fifty people to two thousand people, with new colonies being built throughout New England. Of course, this was just the beginning—the beginning of America's independence from England.

As I walked down the hall, my mind raced thinking about what the next lesson should be! It can't be boring, I thought. Why not just pick up where I left off? Absorbed in my own thinking about exceptional Americans like Benjamin Franklin and Patrick Henry, I was surprised to hear someone say, "Mr. Revere?"

I didn't recognize the voice at first until I looked down the hall and saw the principal's daughter, Elizabeth, in a purple pleated skirt and a pristine white blouse with her hands on her hips. Her long blond hair had been expertly curled and there was a purple headband perfectly placed on the top of her head. She looked surprised to see me and said, "I thought my dad said you weren't coming back? Ugh. I guess this means you're teaching Honors History again."

"Oh, hello, Elizabeth, great to see you," I said in the most positive way I could.

"Don't you have some horse stalls to clean or something? I mean, really!" she said in a feisty tone.

I ignored her insult and while smiling I said, "As a matter of fact, I'm all done cleaning today and was just thinking about my next history lesson. And I do hope you'll choose to be in my class!" Win them over with kindness, I always say! I was determined that this little diva was not going to get the best of me.

Elizabeth huffed and said, "I see you still have your outfit on. You do know it's not Halloween, right? That's not until October, the month *after* September."

I forced a smile on my face and nearly had to bite my tongue so I wouldn't say something I would regret.

She continued her insults and said, "Seriously, the 1700s called and they want their clothes back! In fact, why just send the clothes? You should seriously consider getting a one-way ticket."

Ever so charming, I thought. I took a deep breath and said. "Yes, Paul Revere is still my hero and I must say I like this colonial jacket a lot. I know you don't like me much, but I'd like to propose a peace treaty. Similar to what the Pilgrims proposed with Massasoit and the Pokanoket Indians when they first arrived in the colonies of the New World. What do you say?" I asked.

"I say you are ultra-weird, but whatever floats your boat. I'll be in your class but on my own terms. And don't think for a second that you've fooled me. You may have stumped my father, but I know you're up to something. I'll find out what it is," she said as firmly as ever.

Populations in towns in the American colonies were
growing extremely quickly, as in Lexington, seen here.

"Well, great, that's a start!" I said. I wanted to roll my eyes and tell her she was extremely irritating, but I knew that wouldn't be the best approach. Patience, Revere, patience, I thought.

After saying goodbye to the little darling, I walked down the hall and back toward the football field. That's when I felt my phone buzz. It was a text from Tommy. It said, "So? R u coming back?"

I texted, "Yes, teaching tomorrow!!!! Get ready to meet Ben Franklin!"

Tommy texted, "No way! Sounds amazing! TTWL!"

I texted, "TTWL? You mean, TTYL? Talk to you later?" thinking I was very hip.

Tommy responded, "Nope, I mean TTWL. Time travel with Liberty!!!!!"

I smiled. Yes, I thought. We would definitely need Liberty. It was time to pick him up from the livery. I had better go get him some apples, I thought. The best way to win Liberty over is always through his stomach.

Chapter 2

*T*he *sky darkened* above Manchester Middle School as gusts of wind sent oak leaves cartwheeling over the grass. From inside the classroom I peered through the windows at thick, ominous clouds that seemed to be waiting for just the right moment to douse the school with buckets of water. The Honors History class was the last period of the day and I wondered if Liberty and I would have to travel home in a torrential downpour.

Liberty watched the swirling clouds and said, "Those look like thunderstorm clouds—cumulonimbus to be exact!"

"I'm impressed you know the meteorologist term for this kind of cloud," I said.

Liberty still watched the skies and replied, "After my incident with the lightning I make it a point to know as much as I can about the weather. In particular, how to avoid lightning strikes."

"Maybe it's your electrifying personality that attracts the lightning," I said, smiling.

Liberty turned to me and said with a smirk, "Well, there's not much I can do about that. Some of us are born with an extra dose of charm and charisma."

The school bell rang, which meant that the students would begin arriving in the next few minutes.

"Do you think Elizabeth will return?" Liberty asked.

"I think so. Something tells me she likes keeping me on my toes! She's a handful that one," I said as I double-checked the projector and made sure it was ready to transmit any video footage from my smartphone.

"That's a nice way of putting it. You do remember she tried to fire you as a substitute teacher by catching you with a horse in your classroom? A talking horse!" Liberty winked.

"Yes, but I know the kind of game she's playing," I said. "Elizabeth considers this her school, her territory. My intent wasn't to challenge her authority or remove her from power. Yet she feels threatened by my presence. I imagine it's similar to how the Native Americans felt when the Pilgrims started arriving in the New World. William Bradford befriended the Indians and created peace. It worked for him so I'm going to try to do the same."

I could see that Liberty was thinking about what I had just said and then he replied, "I think some people don't want peace. Instead, they want control. They want people to obey without question. They want to rule with an iron fist. You of all people know that history is full of leaders who were intolerant of others when they tried to stand up for freedom."

"Indeed," I said. "But I consider myself a peacemaker. I'm going to reach out to Elizabeth with peace in mind. The kind of peace that can only come when people or, in this case, students are treated with respect and fairness."

"Well, good luck with that, Mr. Positive!" Liberty said with a grin.

"Wait, that's exactly what we should go over in today's history lesson," I beamed. "By the way, you better disappear for now. After class starts we're going to meet outside for a little scavenger hunt."

"Ooooh, like hunting for Easter eggs?" Liberty said. "I love finding the plastic eggs filled with jelly beans. They are yummy-licious."

"Yes, just like that except we're not hunting for chocolate or eggs. I hid some other cool things outside of the classroom earlier this morning. Kind of a show-and-tell game!" I said.

"Alrighty, I'll meet you outside. But I warn you, the first sound of thunder or the first sight of lightning and I'll be inside faster than you can spell *cumulonimbus*."

"Spell it? I can't even say it!" I said.

"I can," said Tommy, who was the first student to slip into the classroom. He continued, "Cumulonimbus, spelled c-u-m-u-l-o-n-i-m-b-u-s."

"Liberty," I said, "quickly, dematerialize!"

"Oh, that's a good one! D-e-m-a-t- . . ."

"No!" I interrupted, "this isn't a spelling bee. You need to vanish, disappear, dematerialize now! Principal Sherman could come into the classroom at any second!"

"Oh, got it, Captain! See you outside!" Liberty inhaled deeply and disappeared. As long as he held his breath he was invisible.

Tommy laughed and said, "It's hilarious that he calls you *captain*!"

"Yeah, he thinks he's quite amusing," I said.

Tommy walked over to his desk as I walked to the front of the class. Although I had only taught this Honors History class for two days a few weeks ago, I felt completely at home as if I had been there for years. Freedom walked in and went right to her desk at the back of the class. Just before the bell rang, Principal Sherman entered the room followed by a tall and thin African-American boy with a backpack over his shoulder.

"Hey, Cam!" I heard Tommy say as he waved his hand and smiled.

Cam gave Tommy a simple nod and grinned. They seemed to have that best-friend kind of connection where they know what the other is saying with one look. Cam wore a black button-down long sleeve shirt. He wore a dark leather wristband that almost blended in against his dark skin. He appeared at first glance to be a happy kid and he had this look in his eyes, like he knew more than he was telling.

Principal Sherman spoke: "Allow me to make a quick intro-duction. This is Cameron. His family just moved here."

"My mom calls me Cameron, but I like to go by Cam," he said.

"I like to call students by their formal names," said Principal Sherman. "Cameron, this is Mr. Revere. He's teaching temporar-ily until Mrs. Borrington returns. Cameron tells me that history is one of his favorite subjects so I'm sure the two of you will get along splendidly. Now, if you'll excuse me I must get back to my office for another appointment." True to his word, the principal lumbered toward the door and exited.

I noticed all eyes in the classroom were on Cam. I turned to him and said, "Welcome, Cam. Before you take your seat, per-haps you could tell us something about yourself." He looked at me as if to say my clothing was a bit outdated. I noticed he paid particular attention to my boots. Ah, yes, my boots. Very comfortable, I must say.

"Um, okay, sure," Cam said, turning his attention toward the class. He had the kind of smile that felt contagious and lit up the entire room. "Like the principal said, my family just moved here from Colorado. I like to play sports, video games, and build forts with my new neighbor, Tommy." He gave Tommy a nod. He clearly wasn't shy!

"Thank you, Cam," I said. "Welcome to the class. Does anyone have any questions for Cam?"

A girl with curly brown hair asked, "Do you play football for the Lions?"

"No," said Cam, "but I went to the game yesterday and saw Mr. Revere juke out our mascot!"

The class applauded with whooping and hollering.

I raised my hands to quiet the class and said, "Thank you, but I was lucky. If there are no other questions then we'll—"

Suddenly, Tommy raised his hand as if reaching for the ceiling. He looked frantic like he had to go to the bathroom. I responded, "This looks urgent, Tommy. You have a question for Cam or are you going to tell us you have ants in your pants?"

The class laughed and Tommy said, "Touché, Mr. Revere. Nice one. But I wondered if Cam was going to tell us about his fake eye?"

"Tommy," I chastened, "this is hardly the place. Cam, I apologize for—"

"Oh, it's okay," said Cam. "It's no big deal. I pop it out and show people all the time."

Cam brought his cupped hand up to his eye as he dropped his

chin to his chest. He covered his right eye and gently squeezed his eye socket. When he pulled back his hand, his right eye was closed and sure enough, an eyeball sat in the palm of his hand. The only sound came from the wind outside as the students stared in silence.

"Putting it back in is the hard part," he said as he gathered the eyeball between his fingers. "Sometimes it gets slippery and . . . oops!" The eyeball slipped from his fingers and landed on the desk closest to him. As it bounced and rolled across the desktop, the girl sitting at the desk screamed like someone had just dropped a hundred snakes on her lap. In fact, the entire class sounded like they were screaming and gasping and grossing out as the eyeball rolled off the desk, bounced off the floor, and started rolling across the room as feet quickly jumped up and out of the way.

That's when I noticed Cam grinning and Tommy laughing hysterically. In fact, Cam had both eyes open with eyeballs in both sockets. I folded my arms and gave Tommy *the look*. However, it was difficult to keep a serious face. When Tommy saw me he quickly jumped out of his seat, ran toward the eyeball, and scooped it up. More gasps and more "ewwwwwws" as he casually put the eyeball in his pocket and returned to his seat.

When the class finally calmed down, Cam said, "I'm sorry, Mr. Revere. Tommy said you liked practical jokes and promised me you'd be okay with it."

I couldn't help but smile and said, "I think this deserves a round of applause." I started to clap and the students joined me.

"Bravo, Tommy and Cam, for a very convincing performance." Tommy was still giggling, which made Cam start to laugh again. Then Cam said, "It's a classic prank, the ol' *introduce the new guy with the fake eye.*"

Trying desperately not to laugh, Tommy said, "The look . . . on your faces . . . was priceless."

"You know what they say, Tommy. What goes around comes around," I said.

"Yeah, especially a rubber eyeball from the dollar store," Tommy said as he covered his mouth and burst out laughing again.

I'll admit that the laughter and innocent prank put me in a good mood. "All right," I said, still smiling. "Cam, why don't you take that seat in the middle." I pointed to Elizabeth's empty desk. "We may need to shuffle the seating chart later but for now I think we're good."

Cam walked over and settled into his new seat.

"Today we're going to go on a little history scavenger hunt," I said. "I know that it's a little windy outside but it hasn't started raining yet so let's quickly see if we can do this. Let's all walk outside near the back of the school."

After a minute or two we were all outside. It was barely windy and I wondered if this was the calm before the storm.

As I asked for everyone's attention, I saw Liberty suddenly appear behind the students. I continued, "Of course, our class wouldn't be the same without Liberty!" I reached out my hand in Liberty's direction. The class turned around and immediately smothered Liberty with praise and affection. Dozens of hands petted his sides, nose, and mane as they commented how much they missed him. Liberty just stood there like he was taking a long, hot shower.

"That's Mr. Revere's horse," I heard Tommy tell Cam.

Rush Revere's Honors History Class

DEMATERIALIZE

MANCHESTER
MIDDLE SCHOOL

"Sometimes Mr. Revere will sneak him into the classroom. It's a secret so don't tell anyone."

I looked up at the sky and said, "We probably don't have much time. I've hidden six different objects around the school-yard. Each has a bright yellow ribbon tied to it. I'll give you five minutes to search for them and bring them back to me. Ready, set, go!"

"I see one," said a boy from somewhere in the back.

Instantly, all twenty-five students took off running in different directions. The wind had picked up a little but nothing out of the ordinary. Within minutes the students returned.

"Wonderful," I said. "All of the objects have someone in common. Let's see what you've found. Tommy, I believe you returned first. Show us what you have."

Tommy awkwardly stepped forward while wearing a pair of black swimming fins. He waddled like a large penguin.

"Can you tell the class who invented flippers?" I asked.

"Uhhhh, Aquaman?" he said.

The class laughed.

"Strike one," I said.

"Captain Nemo?" he tried again.

More laughter.

"Strike two," I grinned.

Tommy's eyebrows went up and his eyes went wide as he said, "Ohhhhh, I remember now. It's SpongeBob SquarePants!"

Tommy high-fived several of the students near him, including Cam, as the rest of the class laughed.

"You're in fine form today, Tommy," I said with a smile. "How-ever, three strikes and you're out. Who has the next object?"

Freedom stepped forward as Tommy waddled back to the

other students. She said, "I found this old book." She held it up so the other students could see. She sounded a little confused and read the cover, "It says *Gulliver's Travels* by Jonathan Swift."

"Thank you, Freedom," I said. "The book you're holding is a classic. The person who invented the flippers also loved to read and was very smart. Most assuredly, he read *Gulliver's Travels*. In fact, when this book was first published in 1726 the person I'm thinking of was only twenty years old."

"Seventeen twenty-six? Whoa, that's a long time ago!" one boy said.

"So this mystery person was born in 1706?" said Tommy. "That's like eighty-six years from the time the *Mayflower* arrived and the Pilgrims landed at Plymouth Rock."

"Correct," I said.

Several students turned to Tommy and looked surprised by his quick calculation.

"What?" Tommy asked innocently. "It was a lucky guess."

"What else did you find?" I asked.

Cam stepped forward and said, "I found this newspaper. The crazy thing about it is that it's the *Pennsylvania Gazette*, printed in 1732. How did you find a newspaper this old, Mr. Revere?"

"Oh, I have a friend that has a way of getting old things," I said, winking at Liberty. "The person I'm thinking of was also a printer. In fact, his newspaper, the *Pennsylvania Gazette*, was the most successful newspaper in the colonies. Does anyone want to guess the man I'm thinking of?"

Nobody raised their hand.

"Very well, there are three more items. Let's see them all."

Three students came forward, with a piece of wood, a kite, and reading glasses. I briefly described each one. "I'm sure you're wondering what a piece of wood has to do with the history mystery man. Well, in 1742 this man invented a new kind of stove. It was a metal-lined fireplace that stood in the middle of a room. It provided more heat and less smoke than an open fireplace and used less wood. This stove was made from cast iron and would radiate heat from the middle of the room in all directions. This stove was a very popular way to warm your home if you lived in colonial America. In fact, it's still used today."

"What about these crazy-lookin' glasses?" asked a boy who was wearing them and trying to see through the upper and lower lenses.

"Those reading glasses are called bifocals. The man I'm thinking of created them in 1784. The upper half of the glass lens was for distance and the lower half of the lens was for reading."

"My grandma has a pair of those," said Tommy.

"Yeah, right," said Cam, sarcastically. "You know you have a pair, don't lie."

Cam and Tommy joked around as they playfully slugged each other in the arms.

I continued, "Yes, they're still popular even today," I said.

"Did this guy also invent the kite?" asked a girl who held up the red and white diamond-shaped kite with a long blue tail.

"No," I said. "But this person in history used the kite to experiment with electricity. That's a pretty big clue of who I'm thinking of."

"Benjamin Franklin!" said Tommy.

"Bingo!" I said.

"Isn't his face on the one-dollar bill?" asked a redheaded girl.

"Actually, he's on the one-hundred-dollar bill," I corrected.

Benjamin Franklin

"Did you hide one of those somewhere in the schoolyard, too?" asked Tommy.

"I'm a teacher, not a banker," I said with a laugh. "But Tommy is right about Benjamin Franklin. He is the mystery man of history that invented the swimming fins, owned a printing press, and created the Franklin stove. He loved reading so much he established a library. And in 1753 his experiments with electricity enabled him to create a device that could protect homes and buildings from the destructive force of lightning bolts."

"The lightning rod!" shouted Liberty.

He'd been so quiet, I'd almost forgotten that Liberty was with us.

"A very useful device," Liberty explained. "A lightning rod is an iron rod attached to the top of a house or building and connected to a wire that is attached to another rod that's in the ground. Since lightning is typically attracted to the highest point of a building, the electric charge from a lightning bolt will strike the rod and the charge is conducted harmlessly into the ground. I remember now that our large barn back home had one at either end of the roof."

That's when I noticed Cam staring at Liberty with his jaw open.

"Am I seeing things or did that horse just talk?" he mumbled.

Tommy, who was standing beside Cam, said, "Oh, that's right. I should've warned you about that. He's a talking horse."

Cam slugged Tommy in the arm again and laughed, "Whatever! Where I come from the horses don't talk! Nice practical joke!"

Cam was smiling and Tommy looked at me and shrugged like he wasn't sure what to say next.

One of Ben Franklin's most famous inventions—bifocal glasses.

Benjamin Franklin on the front of the U.S. $100 bill.

As a boy in Boston, Benjamin Franklin made a pair of swim fins. In comparison to modern-day swim fins, his version was shaped more like an artist's palette.

"Seriously," Cam continued, "that looked like he was actually talking. That's got to be the best prank ever."

Just then the sky lit up and within a few seconds the sound of thunder made all of us jump. Liberty stepped back and yelled, "I'm out of here!" He bolted away from us and out of sight as he rounded the corner of the school.

"Everyone, please head inside. We don't have much time before the bell rings and class is over. So let's meet back at the classroom and finish up today's lesson."

As we headed back inside, random raindrops started to fall from the sky and by the time we were back inside the classroom the drops had turned to a heavy shower.

The six Franklin objects were placed on the teacher's desk and once everyone had settled in their seats again I said, "We only talked about some of the inventions and discoveries that came from Benjamin Franklin. There were many others. But it's clear that he was devoted to improving life. He was a successful businessman, inventor, scientist, and politician. Why do you think he was so successful?"

"Because he tried new things?" said a boy in the front row.

"True, I'm sure that had something to do with it. Anyone else?" I asked.

"Because he had a wild imagination," said a girl with short hair and freckles.

"Yes, it would certainly take a big imagination to do some of the things he did."

I noticed Freedom raised her hand and I eagerly called on her. She said, "It sounds like he was a hard worker and kept really busy. He wasn't afraid to try new things. And I bet he didn't spend all of his free time playing video games."

I replied, "True! Video games, movies, iPads, smartphones, or any of the electronic things that we spend time with today didn't exist when Benjamin Franklin was alive. Think about how much time kids today spend playing video games or watching TV. Now, these aren't bad things to do but if you used that same amount of time instead to think like Benjamin Franklin, what might you be able to do? What could you create or invent? Your ideas might very well change the world!"

"What's up with Freedom knockin' our video games!" Cam whispered to Tommy. Tommy and Cam fist-bumped and then Cam raised his hand and asked, "That's cool how he invented all that stuff, but wasn't Benjamin Franklin one of the Founding Fathers of America? Didn't he spend a lot of time defending the rights of the colonies?"

"You're absolutely right, Cam," I said. I had forgotten that Cam's favorite subject was history. "In fact, right after Benjamin Franklin invented the lightning rod you could say he was *struck* with an idea to unite the colonies."

"You mean, he had a brain-*storm?*" Tommy said, smiling and reaching out to Cam for another fist bump.

A flash of lightning followed immediately by a loud crack of thunder overhead made everyone jump in their seats. I could hear the heavy rain on the roof of the school.

I brought my attention back to the students and said, "Yes, Tommy, Franklin had a brainstorm. Like I said earlier, Franklin was a smart man. He was a genius. He was passionate about freedom and ready to defend America with his wit and wisdom! And it was the Stamp Act of 1765 that convinced him that it was time to tell England what he really thought."

"What's the Stamp Act?" asked a girl in the front row.

"I'm glad you asked," I said. "Tomorrow, Liberty is going to introduce us to the Stamp Act with a special musical presentation, something you will not want to miss!"

"You mean, Liberty, your horse?" asked Cam.

"Yes. Liberty's a very talented horse. I don't want to give anything away. Just be sure to come tomorrow and you'll be in for a special treat."

Just then, the school bell rang and the students started gathering their backpacks and exiting the room. Freedom, however, came to the front of the classroom. She looked rather panicked and whispered, "Mr. Revere, we have a situation."

"Oh?" I asked. "What seems to be the problem?"

"It's Liberty," she said. "Right after that loud thunderclap I reached out to him with my mind. I sensed he was scared. That lightning and thunder felt like it was right on top of us. Anyway, he's in the teachers' lounge waiting for us."

"That's quite the gift you have, Freedom," I said. "Very convenient. And I wasn't aware that your telepathic ability to speak to animals could reach beyond just a few yards."

"Well, usually, it can't," she said. "But I've grown a strong connection with Liberty so it's easier. In fact, he's learning to speak to my mind as well."

"Well, thank you for telling me," I said sincerely.

Freedom still looked extremely worried as she glanced over her shoulder waiting for the final students to exit the classroom.

"Is there something else you needed to tell me?" I asked, almost afraid to hear what she had to say.

Freedom opened her mouth like she was about to say something but didn't know how to say it.

Benjamin Franklin in his printing shop.

"Just spit it out, Freedom," I said, encouraging her. "It's about Liberty, isn't it?"

She silently nodded. "He's not alone in the teachers' lounge. He's with, um, he's with Benjamin Franklin."

"Excuse me?" I asked, clearly not hearing her correctly.

"Liberty's not sure how it happened," Freedom exclaimed. "One minute he was hiding in the teacher's lounge, hoping there wouldn't be any more lightning. He said that all he could think about was Benjamin Franklin and his invention of the lightning rod. He concentrated really hard and thought that if Ben Franklin were here we'd all be safe. And that's when the lightning flashed right over the school and the next second, BOOM! Benjamin Franklin appeared out of nowhere!"

I stood there staring at Freedom like she was a ghost.

"Mr. Revere," Freedom asked softly. "Did you hear what I said?"

I snapped out of my trance and took a deep breath. I exhaled and asked, "Liberty told you all of this?"

"Yeah, I mean telepathically he did," she said. "And he's really scared that you're going to be mad at him."

"Tell him I'm not mad," I said. Was I stunned? Of course. Worried? Yes. Feeling like the course of world history may have just been altered? Absolutely. "And tell him we're coming to help." I took out my phone and texted Tommy: "Need your help. TTWL. Meet in teachers' lounge ASAP."

May 9, 1754.   NUMB. 1324.

The Pennsylvania  Gazette.

Containing the Freſheſt Ad-   *vices, Foreign and Domeſtick.*

A copy of Franklin's *Pennsylvania Gazette*, May 9, 1754.
His newspaper was the most successful in the colonies.

Chapter 3

*F*reedom and I raced down the hallway to the teachers' lounge. I could still hear the rain coming down outside but thankfully the lightning and thunder had ceased.

When we stopped in front of the door Freedom said, "I better wait out here and keep guard."

"Good idea," I replied. I quickly slipped inside the teachers' lounge. Sure enough, Liberty was standing over a man dressed in colonial clothing who was awkwardly lying on a long orange couch.

"Are you sure you're not angry?" Liberty asked timidly.

"I assure you I'm not mad," I said, forcing a smile. I walked closer to get a better look. The middle-aged man appeared to be unconscious but his face looked surprisingly peaceful. "Whoever this is, he's a dead ringer for Benjamin Franklin," I said.

"You mean he's dead?" Liberty shouted, sounding panicked.

"Who's dead?" Tommy said as he walked into the room. "What the . . . who's that?"

The door opened again and Freedom peeked inside. "You should try and keep it down . . . Wow! So it really is Benjamin Franklin!" She slipped in all the way and put her back to the door.

"Benjamin Franklin!" Tommy exclaimed. "You killed Benjamin Franklin?"

"He's dead?" Freedom panicked.

"Yes! I mean no. I mean I don't know, it all happened so fast!" Liberty whimpered. "I'm going to prison for killing Franklin, aren't I!"

I kneeled down to feel the man's pulse. "He's not dead. But how did he get like this?"

"Like—I told—Freedom," Liberty tried to explain through gasps of anguish and despair. "The lightning flashed, the thunder boomed, and then Mr. Franklin appeared out of nowhere. I think I wished him here."

"Sort of like how you can stop time when you concentrate hard enough," Freedom explained.

"The shock of traveling through time must've been too much for him and he passed out," Tommy said.

"I was close enough to push him onto the couch. He almost collapsed onto the floor. That must count for something, right?" Liberty said pleadingly.

For the first time I looked closely at the face of the supposed Benjamin Franklin. He had wrinkles in his broad forehead and under his eyes. He had a large head and the little hair he had was blond but graying. His leather shoes, cream stockings, and sea-green breeches and coat were clean but somewhat plain. For the first time the realization that I was kneeling above the legendary Benjamin Franklin hit me like a ton of bricks.

"What's in his hand?" Tommy asked.

In his left hand were several pieces of parchment with cursive writing on them. I quickly browsed the pages and after reading several sentences a sense of panic overcame me. "Oh my," I gasped.

"What's wrong?" Freedom asked.

"This appears to be notes for a speech. If I'm correct, we may have just snatched away Benjamin Franklin before he could persuade the English government to repeal the Stamp Act."

"And that's a bad thing, right?" Liberty worried.

"I don't know yet," I said. "What I do know is that we have to get him back to the past immediately. Lucky for us it doesn't appear that he's completely aware of what's happened. Let's try to get Mr. Franklin onto Liberty's saddle. Liberty, move over here so it's easier for us to hoist him up."

As Liberty moved his large equine body, someone tried to enter the teacher's lounge. The door pushed open only a few inches and Freedom pushed back to close it. "Hey! Open the door," Elizabeth yelled. "I saw Freedom go in there and I've been listening to your conversation. Let me in!"

Liberty backed up to the door and helped Freedom keep it shut.

"What do we do?" Freedom whispered.

"We stick with our plan," I softly said. "Tommy, Freedom, on the count of three we lift Mr. Franklin onto the saddle. Liberty, keep that door shut."

"That I can do!" Liberty said firmly.

"Hey! I said open the door! I can wait out here all day if I have to," Elizabeth threatened. "I know I heard Mr. Revere and his circus horse. And I'm pretty sure I heard Tommy's voice, too. And from the sound of it some dead guy named Franklin. So I'm going to give you thirty seconds to open the door. After that, I'm bringing my dad and you know how big he is. He'll have this door open in no time!"

As Elizabeth finished speaking we adjusted Franklin's body onto the saddle and I slipped on behind him.

"I'll try and be back in a flash," I said.

"We can't let Elizabeth catch us in here," Tommy said.

"Um, she already has," Freedom whispered matter-of-factly.

"No, she hasn't," Tommy replied. "Technically, she only saw you come in."

"She said she heard our voices," Freedom said.

"Well, when she only finds you in here she'll think again," Tommy said, smiling.

"So you're leaving me here?" Freedom whispered with wide eyes.

"It'll be worse if Elizabeth finds all of us together," Tommy pointed out. "If she just finds you, well, just tell her you were sleepwalking and ended up in the teachers' lounge."

"Sleepwalking?" Freedom shook her head. "That's a lame excuse."

"You'll think of something," Tommy said.

Freedom sighed, "Fine, just go. I'll figure it out."

"Do we have enough room to time-jump in this small room?" Tommy asked.

I hesitated and said, "Well, we've never tried it with this much space but—"

"I can do it," Liberty interrupted. "I'll do anything to get us out of this mess."

I turned to Tommy and said, "You'll need to jump right behind us. We're headed to England, 1765!"

Tommy raised his eyebrows and said with a smile, "Cool."

"Let's go, Liberty," I said.

In his loudest whisper, Liberty said, *"Rush, rush, rushing to history!"*

Like before, the circular portal of swirling purple and gold instantly began to open. I held tightly to Liberty's saddle and Benjamin Franklin and said, "London, England, 1765, let's return Benjamin Franklin to the Palace of Westminster." With a hop, skip, and a jump Liberty bolted up and through our door to the past.

As we landed the jolt caused Benjamin Franklin to stir. Groggily, he began to come to.

"Quickly," I said, "help me get him to the ground."

With Tommy's help we lowered him to a freshly cut lawn. Immediately, I noticed a heavy fog that surrounded us. I couldn't see much but I could hear the distant sound of horses. Yes, in fact I could see a faint outline of two horses pulling a carriage. Large trees bordered a nearby dirt road that disappeared into a fog bank.

"Who are you?" Benjamin asked as he looked up at me from the grass.

"Let me help you up, Mr. Franklin," I said with eagerness. I grabbed Ben's hand and pulled him to his feet.

He stood, brushed himself off, and said, "I'm afraid I'm a bit disoriented. I was riding in a carriage and on my way to give a

speech to Parliament and then . . ." He paused. "Let me think, oh yes, there was a brilliant white light and for a second I remember staring at . . . at a horse." He turned his head and stared at Liberty. He pointed, "That horse!"

I tried to divert his attention and loudly exclaimed, "Benjamin Franklin! You really are Benjamin Franklin! It's a great honor, sir. You're a legend. An American hero. And we're standing here! With you! Right now! Talking. With you." He was a very big deal back then. It's sort of like running into the president! Not exactly, but a big deal.

"I don't think we've met, sir," said Benjamin. "You seem to know my name and though I'm flattered by your compliments I'm afraid I've much more to accomplish in my life to ever be called any of the things you've mentioned. So, tell me, what is your name? And who is this fine young man with you?"

I was giddy at the sight of one of the Founding Fathers of the United States of America. He was shorter than I was, probably about five feet nine or ten inches, but he was larger than life! Standing right in front of me! He put me at ease as he smiled and waited for my response.

When I continued staring, Tommy grabbed my arm and shook it a little, "Mr. Revere? This is the part where you introduce yourself."

I snapped out of my momentary dream and then realized it wasn't a dream. Benjamin Franklin was actually speaking to me. I took a deep breath and said, "Yes, of course, I'm Rush Revere, history teacher and fellow American."

"Ah, yes," said Benjamin. "I thought you might be from the thirteen colonies as your accent sounds a little non-British."

Franklin as chief of the Union Fire Company of Philadelphia—
the first volunteer fire department in Philadelphia.

"Oh, yes," I said, laughing, still feeling a little lightheaded. "I'm from the United States of America."

"Pardon me, the united what?" asked Benjamin.

Tommy whispered, "Mr. Revere, the United States hasn't been invented yet, remember?"

"What an interesting thought," Benjamin said. "I'll have to try and remember that."

I composed myself and said, "It truly is a great honor to meet you. I apologize for sounding like a bumbling idiot." I turned to Tommy and said, "This is one of my students, Tommy."

Liberty cleared his throat for attention and sidestepped close.

"Oh, and, of course, this is Liberty," I said with a little bit of apprehension. I was worried that Liberty's enthusiasm to meet any historical figure, especially one from his own century, might cause him to forget our secret that he was a talking horse. And just like I suspected, he forgot.

"It's a great honor, Mr. Franklin, I'm just glad you're not dead," said Liberty with great enthusiasm.

"Fascinating," said Benjamin as he began to closely examine Liberty like he was an exhibit at the Museum of Natural History. "Absolutely fascinating!"

"Oh, yes," Liberty continued. "You can't begin to know the relief I felt when I found out you were still alive! Whew! Seriously, seeing you standing here brings me a lot of joy! Yes, sir. Joy with a capital J."

Benjamin looked into Liberty's mouth and then into his ears and nose. He finally said, "I'm thoroughly impressed. It appears you have the ability to reason and can fluently speak the English language." He turned to me and asked, "Is this an invention of your doing?"

The Library Company of Philadelphia was founded by Benjamin Franklin in 1731.

The First American political cartoon, published in 1754 by Benjamin Franklin in his *Pennsylvania Gazette* to rally the former colonies against British rule.

I gave the best explanation I could. "Yes, well, it was a crazy experiment with lightning," I replied nervously. "Sort of an accident. Impossible to duplicate. But I've nurtured Liberty and helped him adjust to his new abilities and intellect."

"Well, I must commend you for the scientific success that you have achieved," said Benjamin. "Truly, I feel very fortunate to have witnessed your accomplishment. But you would be wise to keep Liberty's gift a secret. I am all for sharing the inventions I have discovered, but your discovery is a . . . a . . . a natural phenomenon! Yes, definitely a wonder to behold!"

Liberty blushed and said, "Ahh, shucks. Thanks, Frankaben, I mean, Benjafrank, I mean, Franklin Benjamin. Doh, I mean, Benjamin Franklin, sir." Liberty blushed, again.

Benjamin stroked Liberty's neck and said, "Yes, Liberty, you are definitely one of a kind. Indeed, most people would pass out in shock at the discovery of a talking horse!"

"Thank you for your counsel," I said. "And Liberty is usually very careful about letting others know about his gift. Aren't you, Liberty?"

"Oh, uh, yes," said Liberty. "But I knew you'd understand, Mr. Franklin. I had a good feeling about you."

"We're just glad we found you when we did! Aren't we, Mr. Revere," Tommy said.

"Definitely! And I'm sure we've taken too much of your time. Certainly, you're here in England for a special reason," I hinted.

"I almost forgot," Benjamin said as he quickly looked at his pocket watch. "What a relief," he sighed. "It appears that time is on my side today."

Time is always on our side with Liberty, I thought.

"As fellow colonists you should join me," said Benjamin. "As a colonial representative of Pennsylvania I've been invited to testify to Parliament about what is happening in the colonies, particularly about the opposition to the Stamp Act. I believe if we cut across this lawn we can hail a carriage."

As we followed Benjamin I found myself smiling at the mere fact that we were about to experience an important moment in American history. It appeared that the fog was thinning and in the distance loomed a massive building that looked like a castle fortress.

"Mr. Franklin," Tommy said. "Are you in trouble? Why do you have to testify? Was there a crime? And what's Parliament? Sorry to ask so many questions."

Benjamin laughed and said, "Asking questions is the first step to discovery! Let me answer your questions in reverse. Parliament is the word we use in England for the English government. King George III regularly meets with Parliament—the House of Lords and the House of Commons—to make rules and laws to govern his people."

Tommy asked, "Do the King and Parliament make the rules for the thirteen colonies, too?"

"Yes," said Benjamin, "and that's beginning to be a problem. In fact, many colonists think it's a crime for the King to tax the colonies. In particular, I have come to testify to members of Parliament why the colonies dislike the Stamp Act so much."

"I remember Mr. Revere mentioned the Stamp Act in our history class," said Tommy.

Liberty cleared his throat and said, "You'd know what the Stamp Act is if you'd seen and heard my Stomp Act!" Liberty said. "I'd perform it for you now but it's just not the same without the music."

"I am still not accustomed to a talking horse," Benjamin said with a chuckle. "Please excuse my laughter. It is simply an expression of surprise and admiration. Are you suggesting that you can also sing?"

"Oh boy, let's not encourage him," I cringed.

"I'm not prepared to sing my Stamp Act song just yet but the national anthem is one of my favorites." At once, Liberty began singing, "*O! say does that star-spangled banner yet wave, o'er the land of the free! And the home of the brave!*"

Benjamin Franklin applauded and said, "I am amazed. And please be assured that your secret is safe with me. However, I am not familiar with this national anthem."

I quickly replied, "Oh, yes, well, it hasn't caught on just yet."

"I think it has potential," Benjamin said. "I especially like the part about the *land of the free and home of the brave*. In fact, it describes America perfectly. Our forefathers who first settled in America from England are some of the bravest people I have ever read about. Men like William Bradford, for example."

"Our class learned all about William Bradford and Myles Standish, who sailed on the *Mayflower* and settled Plymouth Plantation!" Tommy exclaimed.

Benjamin nodded and said, "We owe everything to the brave colonists who first came to America to start a land of the free. And now it is my turn to be brave by fighting for the rights of the thirteen colonies. We can talk more inside the carriage."

Several carriages waited in a row like taxis ready to take people to various destinations in London. Neatly trimmed hedges bordered either side of the road. The grass, the shrubs, the trees were perfectly landscaped. It was a sign that England was an established land with centuries of tradition and order. We waited for a carriage to pass before crossing the road.

Benjamin called to the coachman of the lead carriage with two white horses and said, "Westminster Palace, the House of Commons, please."

The footman opened the small door and Benjamin paid him before we stepped up and inside the enclosed interior. Two purple velvet benches faced each other. Benjamin Franklin sat on one side and Tommy and I sat on the other. I saw Liberty roll his eyes. He was always bothered by the fact that he couldn't fit inside cars or buses and now, carriages.

As the carriage rumbled down the dirt road, I looked out the side window to see Liberty prancing alongside the horses pulling the carriage. From the looks of it he had forgotten about riding inside the carriage and was now flirting like he was a stallion.

Tommy announced, "Wow, this is really bumpy! This carriage could use a pair of shock absorbers."

"I am not familiar with shock absorbers as you say," said Benjamin.

"Oh, it's a device to help smooth out the ride so it's not so bumpy."

"Are you an inventor, Tommy?" Benjamin asked.

"I do like to build things. Do you have any advice for me?" Tommy asked.

"Never let uncertainty or fear stop you. If you work hard and think big you can accomplish anything, especially in a free land like America. There are people that will tell you otherwise. They will say you are not good enough. You are not old enough. You are not smart enough. Balderdash! Do not listen to them. If you have a dream, follow it!"

A view some years later, Hanover Square in London, 1787.

"Thanks!" Tommy said. "I'll remember that. By the way, you said you were fighting for the rights of the colonies. Exactly what rights are you fighting for?"

"I'm fighting against this horrible idea called the Stamp Act. Horrible it is, horrible! Last year, the British prime minister, George Grenville, passed the Stamp Act, the first direct tax on the American colonies."

"I know all about taxes," said Tommy matter-of-factly. "Last year I saved my money to buy this awesome Lego set and—"

"I'm sorry to interrupt," said Benjamin, "but what is a Lego set? I've been gone from the colonies for a couple of years. Is this some kind of new toy?"

"Um, yeah," Tommy said reluctantly. "They're sort of like building blocks but they have pieces that connect together and you can build all kinds of things. I have this Lego set with instructions to build the Death Star, you know, from *Star Wars* and—"

"Tommy has quite the imagination," I said, cutting in laughing as I nudged Tommy.

"Instructions to build a star of death? For children? Interesting," mused Benjamin.

"Anyway," Tommy continued, "I knew the exact price of this Lego set because I wrote it down and looked at it every week. I did lots of chores and worked hard and saved my money. When I had earned enough my mom took me to the store to purchase it. I put the exact change on the counter but the salesperson said it wasn't enough. I'm really good at numbers so I knew I wasn't wrong. That's when my mom told me that I'd forgotten about the tax. I thought, the what? The sales tax, she said. And that's when I learned that we pay a little extra on everything we buy and that little extra money, the sales tax, goes back to the government."

"And tell me, Tommy, how did this tax make you feel?" Benjamin Franklin asked.

"Well, at first I didn't think it was fair, but then she said if we all pay a sales tax then that money goes to help run the city. She said this way everyone can enjoy things like public schools, libraries, highways, and police and fire protection. Once I realized all the places and services I get to enjoy because of all the taxes that are collected, I really didn't mind paying a little bit every time I buy something."

"You are a very smart boy, Tommy," said Benjamin. "But what if the money from those taxes wasn't used to build up your city or bless its citizens? What if your tax money was being used for something you didn't agree with? What if there was no real benefit to anyone at all?"

Tommy thought for a second and said, "Well, um, wouldn't that be stealing? That doesn't seem fair."

"And that's why the colonists are angry," I said.

"Yes," said Benjamin. "The Stamp Act is making the colonists pay extra money on something they didn't vote for. It is a tax that gives nothing back to the community. And we believe it is something that Parliament is doing to undercut our businesses and the success we are having."

"But why do they call it the Stamp Act? I don't get it?" asked Tommy.

"It is called the Stamp Act because a stamp is placed on all paper products reminding the colonists that England is still in charge," said Benjamin.

"You mean I have to pay a tax on anything I buy made from paper?" Tommy asked again.

Benjamin replied, "Anything and everything! Newspapers,

almanacs, pamphlets, legal documents of all kinds, ships' papers, licenses, and even playing cards. The act was to be enforced by stamp agents with severe penalties for any who would not pay. However, the colonists are putting a stop to it. Many resist paying the stamp tax. I would not be surprised if someday they rebel against the Empire."

Tommy laughed and said, "That sounds a lot like *Star Wars*."

"Well, I'm not familiar with a *star* war," said Benjamin, "but if the thirteen colonies continue to rebel and resist, it is just a matter of time before the empire strikes back!"

"That's exactly what happens in *Star Wars*!" Tommy shouted. "And then the rebels are forced to retreat until the return of the Jedi!"

I forced a nervous laugh and said, "Ha! Jedi! That's Tommy's special word for hero! Isn't it, Tommy?"

"Oh, um, yeah," Tommy said. "That's right. I made it up. Jedi heroes like William Bradford and Myles Standish! All they wanted was freedom! We can't let them down."

"No worries, Tommy," I said. "I saw colonists in Boston burning anything that had a tax stamp on it. And I've read about how the colonists are threatening the stamp agents. I even heard that one agent was tarred and feathered for trying to enforce the Stamp Act."

Tommy's eyes went wide and asked, "When you say 'tarred and feathered' do you mean . . ."

"I am afraid so," said Benjamin. "It is a barbaric and cruel act to slop hot tar on someone's body and then pour goose feathers on top of them."

"Oh, wow," Tommy said. "This is really getting serious."

As the carriage slowed Benjamin looked out the window and

said, "We have arrived at the Palace of Westminster. And it appears that the fog has lifted."

In 1765, England was said to be the most powerful country in the world and as I peered out the window I saw that the Palace of Westminster was certainly reflective of that power. The massive stone building, originally built in the Middle Ages, had several tall, castle-like structures that overlooked the River Thames. A beautiful courtyard landscaped with well-trimmed shrubs and trees welcomed us. The overall site was breathtaking.

The carriage stopped and as the door opened Benjamin said, "Follow me, gentlemen. I am honored to have you as my guests."

As we exited the carriage I turned to Tommy and whispered, "This building is where the British lords and lawmakers come to govern. In the United States, the Capitol building in Washington, D.C., is the equivalent."

In the courtyard that surrounded the steps leading to two ornately carved doors were dozens of men. I assumed these were the lords and lawmakers of England. They were dressed in the finest waistcoats, vests, and breeches. Most wore white wigs or their hair was pulled back and tied off with a ribbon.

The sound of a large bell rung through the plaza and the men responded by filing into the palace doors.

"Now, let's see if I can get these British gents to repeal the Stamp Act!" said Benjamin as we followed him into the Palace.

We were the last ones to enter the building, so Liberty took a deep breath and slipped in behind us like he was wearing an invisibility cloak.

Chapter 9

*B*enjamin *sat in* a wooden chair behind a well-crafted wooden desk in the middle of a large room. On the walls, masterful oil paintings of former British monarchs hung in grandiose golden frames. Exquisitely carved half columns stood against the walls and reached up to a high ceiling. Three hundred seventy members of Parliament sat in theater seating on either side listening to Franklin's testimony about the colonies' reaction to the Stamp Act. Without question, Benjamin Franklin looked exhausted after answering more than 170 questions. He took another sip of water and waited for another member of Parliament to ask yet another question. Secretively, I continued to record the proceedings with my smartphone.

"He's not being questioned, he's being interrogated," Tommy whispered from the back of the room. "I feel really bad for him. He's got to be really tired."

The House of Commons in session in 1710.

"Remember that he is fighting for freedom. Some people fight for it on the battlefield and some fight for it in a court of law," I said.

"Well, it just goes to show how smart he is. These guys in Parliament keep trying to mess with his mind. It's like they keep asking the same questions to see if he'll give different answers," Tommy said.

"Yes, some lawyers and politicians can be very crafty. I don't think they realize who they are dealing with," I said, softly.

"No kidding. I'd totally pick him to be on my debate team," said Tommy with a big grin.

"What did I miss?" asked Liberty, who suddenly appeared behind a large curtain in the back of the stuffy room. Liberty was present for the first thirty minutes of questioning but then disappeared to find a snack.

"They just passed a law that gives donkeys special privileges over horses," Tommy whispered to Liberty.

"What!" shouted Liberty. The word reverberated off the walls and ceiling. Thankfully, it was difficult to know where the sound was coming from.

"Order!" said the prime minister, who acted as the judge and pounded his gavel. "We will have order during the questioning. Next question."

Another member of Parliament raised his hand and asked, "If the Stamp Act is not repealed, what do you think will be the consequences? How will the people of America respond?"

Benjamin sighed but calmly replied, "A total loss of respect and affection for Great Britain."

Another question came from the other side of the room. "Do you think the people of America would submit to pay the stamp tax if it were moderated?"

Again, Benjamin replied, "No, never, unless compelled by force of arms."

Still another question: "Do they realize the British Empire owes a lot of money to those who helped us fight the French and Indian War—a war that was fought on American soil? Do you think it right that America should be protected by this country and pay no part of the expense?"

Without flinching Benjamin replied, "The colonies raised, clothed, and paid nearly twenty-five thousand men and spent millions during the French and Indian war. Candidly, they believe they have paid their part in full."

"One final question for Mr. Franklin," called the prime minister. "We have heard that the Americans claim 'No taxation without representation.' The fact is Parliament has the right to tax the colonies with or without their consent. Can anything less than a military force carry the Stamp Act into execution?"

Benjamin Franklin smiled the most convincing smile he could give and said with boldness, "I do not see how a military force can be applied to that purpose."

Murmurs spread across the great room and echoed off the walls.

"Why may it not?" asked the prime minister.

"Suppose a military force is sent into America. They will find nobody in arms. What are they to do? They cannot force a man to take stamps who chooses to do without them. They will not find a rebellion. They may, indeed, make one."

More murmuring rippled through the large hall and Benjamin Franklin took a deep breath and exhaled. The prime minister stood from his seat, pounding his gavel, and the meeting was adjourned.

"Let's sneak out to the courtyard and wait for Mr. Franklin," I said.

As we walked outside and down the stone walkway I was reminded again how beautiful London was. The courtyard was circular and symmetrical, with a round pond in the middle. A variety of perfectly pruned shrubs and bushes lined a variety of pathways. We walked to the center of the courtyard and Tommy said, "No wonder the Revolutionary War happened. There's no way England and America are going to agree. They both think they're right. And both sides are getting angrier and angrier. This is not going to end well."

"You're right," I said. "The Stamp Act may very well have been the spark that led to America's independence from England. The King and Parliament won't back down. The thirteen colonies are standing firm for freedom. And tempers will eventually reach a boiling point!"

"Speaking of boiling point," Liberty said, "I think most people overcook their food. There's nothing worse than overcooked potatoes or carrots or especially asparagus! Seriously, limp and soggy asparagus is almost as bad as a limp and soggy hand-shake."

Confused, I questioned, "a soggy handshake?"

Liberty clarified: "You don't want one, trust me. It begins by soaking in the bathtub or playing in a pool for too long and then your hand looks old and wrinkly! Shaking a soggy hand feels like you're holding a slimy, shriveled piece of seaweed. And you're not going to impress anyone with seaweed. Why are we even talking about this?"

I said defensively, "Because when I said boiling point you starting talking about—"

Liberty interrupted. "What we should be talking about is how to help the colonists defend their freedoms!"

I rolled my eyes and said, "I agree. Tommy, do you have any questions about what you heard in there?"

"Yeah, I do," Tommy said. "I'm not sure I understood what *No taxation without representation* means."

"It's the main reason why the colonists are mad," I said. "It's important to understand that the thirteen colonies are still a part of England. They still consider King George to be their king, and they are subject to the rules and laws of the British Empire. So, of course, if they have to live by these laws then they want to help make the laws. Instead, the King and Parliament are making decisions without them."

"You mean like the Stamp Act," said Tommy.

"Exactly! The colonies petitioned Parliament to repeal the stamp tax several times but were ignored each time. Finally, the colonies said, 'no more.' No taxation without representation."

Tommy nodded and said, "It sort of reminds me of this kid named Billy who lived in our neighborhood and had this really cool fort. But he only let the kids on his street play in his fort. I heard it was really cool. It had a pinball machine, and this balloon launcher, and this awesome rope swing! Plus, it had jars full of candy and snacks. Anyway, the kids on my street decided we should make our own cool fort but Billy didn't like that idea. He had a top-secret meeting with the kids on his street and they decided that we could use Billy's fort if we paid to get in. We told him no way, Jose!"

"I thought you said his name was Billy," said Liberty.

"It is," I said. "Jose is just a nickname that rhymes with way."

"Oh," Liberty replied. "You mean like, go take a hike, Mike. Or take a chill pill, Phil. Or go ride a ferret, Garrett!"

"Exactly," Tommy said, laughing. "Anyway, we told Billy that we were going to have our own meeting. We decided we didn't need his lousy fort and we built our own."

"You did just what the colonies did," I said. "They had their own meeting in October 1765. The colonies formed the Stamp Act Congress to figure out what to do and say to England about the Stamp Act."

"I know what I would do," said Liberty. "I would get a big piece of tape and make a line down the center and say this side of the barn is mine and that side of the barn is yours, and if you step on my side of the line then I'm telling Mom! Seriously, I had this brother that was soooo bossy and he thought he owned every inch of our barn and he was—"

I stroked Liberty's neck and said, "It's all right, Liberty. That was in the past. But you bring up a very good point. King George felt like he was the boss of the colonists. He felt like he owned their land and did not want to give it up! That's why he started taxing the people and tried forcing them to buy British products. He was trying to control what they did. He wanted them to think of the British Empire first."

"That's hard to do when you live three thousand miles away," said Tommy.

"The King believed there was lots of money to be made in the colonies," I said. "America was rich in resources like wood, minerals, furs, and especially land. Plus, he sent a lot of British citizens to colonize the New World. You can understand why he was selfish and wanted to maintain his power and make the people feel dependent on England."

"But the colonists are becoming so successful that they really don't need the King or the British Empire, right?" Tommy asked.

"Correct," I said. "America is like a child who is big enough to ride a bike without training wheels. But the King doesn't want to take the training wheels off!"

"Hey, there's Benjamin Franklin," Tommy said pointing.

Sure enough, Benjamin slowly walked out of the Palace of Westminster. He looked like he could use a long nap. We joined him at the center of the courtyard.

"You were amazing in there," said Tommy. "It was like the battle of the minds. Just like when Professor Xavier from the X-Men uses his mind power to fight off the bad guys. Seriously, you're like an eighteenth-century X-Man!"

"Your imagination astounds even me," said Benjamin. "What exactly is an X-Man?"

"Only the coolest group of superheroes to ever exist. Their whole purpose is to fight for and protect our freedoms. Yep, Benjamin Franklin is definitely an X-Man!"

"I have been called a lot of things, but never an X-Man," Benjamin said, laughing.

"I believe you persuaded Parliament to repeal the Stamp Act," I said.

"You must be an optimist," said Benjamin with a wide grin. "Only time will tell. But I want to thank you for your support and for the service you rendered me."

"Thanks, Mr. Franklin, for all your advice. I'll never forget you," Tommy said.

Benjamin put both hands on Tommy's shoulders and said, "Tommy, you are the future of America. I'm an old man and today I feel even older. But when I hear your questions and see the light in your eyes I realize your mind is not much different than mine. Creating new inventions or fulfilling your dreams is

Benjamin Franklin presenting the concerns of the American colonists to the Lord's Council, Whitehall Chapel, London.

simply connecting the dots in your mind. Some ideas have lots of dots and others just a few. But it is all the same process. Dot by dot by dot. The key is to keep going until you reach the final dot. When you do, you will have accomplished something. And with a mind like yours, I know it will be something great!"

Finally, he turned to Liberty and said, "And how could I forget you!"

Liberty smiled and just stood there beaming!

Benjamin placed his hand under Liberty's muzzle and said, "There is no such thing as coincidence, Liberty. God knows where every lightning bolt strikes, if you know what I mean." He winked. "Something tells me you are exactly who you were meant to be. Don't ever forget that."

Liberty's lip quivered just a bit and if he could have I know he would've given Benjamin Franklin a great big horse hug.

"Thank you, again, my friends," said Benjamin. "And when you're back in the colonies if you ever have a chance to meet Patrick Henry I would highly recommend it. I think he's an exceptional American and one of your X-Men," he said, winking at Tommy. "I hope our paths cross again someday." And with that he tipped his hat and we parted ways.

"This was way better than I expected," said Tommy.

"No kidding," said Liberty. "He called you Mr. Future of America! Wow, you're pretty important. I think you should get a T-shirt with 'Mr. Future of America' printed on it."

"Thanks, Liberty, for being my number-one fan," said Tommy. "But I think we should keep this a secret between you and me."

"No problem," Liberty said, grinning. "Now we both have secrets. It's like we're secret members of a secret club of secrets!"

"I hate to break up your secret meeting, but it's time to

time-jump back to Manchester Middle School." I scanned the courtyard and said, "Let's walk over to that tall hedge. It should conceal our departure. Oh, and Liberty, we can't return to the teachers' lounge because we don't know if Elizabeth is still there."

"I hope Freedom is okay," Tommy said.

"I'm more worried about Elizabeth," I said. "I've seen her taunt and tease and insult Freedom over and over again. That kind of thing can be very taxing on a person. One of these days Freedom is going to reach her boiling point just like the colonies. I would not want to be Elizabeth when that happens."

"I say we jump back to the classroom. It should still be empty since school just ended," Liberty said.

"Just ended? It feels like that was days ago," Tommy sighed.

"Good idea, Liberty. The classroom it is," I said.

We traveled to the nearby hedge, and after making sure we were alone, Liberty opened the time portal and we jumped back to the classroom.

"Now I know how Liberty feels. I'm starving," said Tommy as he dismounted from Liberty.

"You see," said Liberty, "I'm not the only one with a big appetite."

"Thanks, again, Mr. Revere," said Tommy. "I better get home." He took off his layer of colonial clothes and put them in his backpack. "I like keeping my modern-day clothes underneath. It's so much easier to change! See ya!" He smiled and quickly left the classroom.

Liberty smiled and said, "So what's the plan, Stan? Should we get something to eat, Pete?"

I tried not to laugh and said, "Good idea."

"Really?" asked Liberty.

"Absolutely," I said. "We need to keep your energy up. We have more time traveling to do!"

When the school bell rang the next day, the students were still busy talking about the previous day's events.

"Good afternoon, class," I said. The class fell silent and I continued: "Today you're going to watch a video I recently edited where Benjamin Franklin defends the rights of the thirteen colonies and asks members of the British Parliament to repeal the Stamp Act. As you watch this video it will be very easy to imagine what it was like to actually be there. While the documentary is playing I'm going to slip out to get my horse, Liberty. As promised, Liberty is going to perform for you his stomp act about the Stamp Act. I'm going to need a couple of volunteers to help me carry in a sound system for Liberty's performance."

Several hands shot up in the air. I looked for three specific students to help me but only saw two of them. I wonder where Freedom is, I thought.

"Tommy and Cam," I said, pointing to the two boys, "please join me in the hallway. The rest of you can sit back and enjoy the show. Oh, I almost forgot." I pulled open my bottom desk drawer and pulled out a bag of bubble gum and another bag of lollipops. "You're welcome to a treat while watching the movie!"

The students eagerly passed around the bags of treats. I walked to the back of the class, dimmed the lights, and started the video projector. I slipped out the door and into the hall, where Cam was waiting for me.

"Where's Tommy?" I asked.

Before Cam could respond, Tommy slipped out of the

classroom door and joined us. He tossed a couple of pieces of bubble gum to Cam.

"Thanks," Cam said as he caught both pieces in his hands.

"Is Cam going to jump with us today?" Tommy said as he tossed an unwrapped piece of gum in his mouth.

I smiled and said, "He can if he wants to."

"Did you say jump? Aren't we just getting the sound system?" Cam asked. "I'll admit, I'm curious to see what your horse does. It looks so real when he moves his lips. It's like he's really talking. I assume the sound system is what you use for the lip sync?"

Tommy looked Cam right in the eyes and without a single sign of a smirk he said, "Cam, this is going to be tough to believe and it might blow your mind, but you've got to trust me on this. Here's the thing, a talking horse is just the tip of the iceberg. Mr. Revere has discovered how to time-travel."

We stood there in silence as Cam carefully stared at us. Finally, he said, "You guys are serious?"

Tommy nodded and looked at me.

"It's true," I said. "There's really only one way to prove it to you. Would you care to join us outside? Liberty is waiting for us there."

"Okay, sure, I'll play along," said Cam. "And I bet there's a flying pig out there, too!"

"Just don't freak out too much, okay?" said Tommy.

"Whatever," Cam said. "Let's go find your magical horse. You probably have a leprechaun in your pocket and a genie in your locker."

"Don't be ridiculous," Tommy smiled. "Leprechauns hate pockets and a genie is way too powerful to keep captive in a locker!"

Tommy thought he was being funny as he laughed at his own joke. I was amused that Tommy thought he was funny. But Cam only gave a courtesy smile as he followed us outside to join Liberty.

"So, where's your horse?" Cam asked.

"Right here!" Liberty said as he appeared directly behind Cam. Cam jumped forward like he had just stepped on hot coals. "Whoa! Man, you have got to teach me how to do this prank!"

"His name is Liberty," I said. "Liberty, this is Cam and we've told him about your secret."

"Which secret?" Liberty asked. "Oh, you mean the time I hid inside Disneyland just before the park closed? I had always wanted to do that. Of course, it's not hard to hide when you can turn invisible but I thought it would be a lot more fun after hours when everyone was gone. Not so much. All the rides are closed and there's nothing to eat so I just wandered through Adventureland and Frontierland and Fantasyland and—"

"Liberty," I said, "I was referring to your time-travel secret."

"Ohhhhhhh," Liberty said with renewed interest. "*That* secret!"

Cam had his mouth open and was staring intently at Liberty.

"You really shouldn't stare with your mouth open," Liberty said. "No offense, but it's sort of rude."

Cam shut his mouth and then opened it and said, "He really can talk."

"Before we go anywhere, Tommy and Cam need these," I said. Opening my travel bag, I pulled out two pairs of colonial clothing.

"Okay, sure, why not." Cam laughed. "I'll play along."

The boys quickly dressed and transformed into eighteenth-century lads.

"Do I look as funny as you do?" Cam asked Tommy.

"Yep," Tommy said. "You should wear those clothes to school."

"No kidding!" Cam laughed. "These breeches and stockings are total girl magnets."

"Make sure you tuck in your shirts," I said.

"Thanks, Mom," Tommy said with a wink.

In an effort to hurry us along I said, "Tommy, why don't you climb up onto Liberty's saddle. I was going to have Freedom ride first but . . . speaking of Freedom, where is she today?"

"Oh, she had a dentist appointment," Tommy said. "But she said she was coming back for Liberty's stomp act."

"Good to know," I said. "Cam, why don't you climb up behind Tommy."

"Um, okay, sure," said Cam.

"Where are we going this time?" Tommy asked.

Cam started laughing. "Wait, wait, wait, this is all kinds of whacked-out. Are you saying that Liberty is how you time-travel?"

"Just hold on tight to the saddle," I said. "Liberty, we're ready!"

"*Rush, rush, rushing to history!*" Liberty said as he galloped forward.

A purple and gold whirlpool swirled in front of us as the time portal opened. I called out, "America, the colony of Virginia, 1765, Patrick Henry." As Liberty, Tommy, and Cam jumped through I followed closely behind. Just before I jumped I saw Elizabeth step out from behind the corner of the school. Only ten yards away, she started running toward the time portal, too. She wouldn't dare jump through after me, would she? In another second I was through the portal and landed in a darkened alley. Liberty, Tommy, and Cam were waiting for me. I stopped and turned back toward the portal, waiting, heart racing, eyes tracing the purple and gold to see if anyone else had time-jumped.

Chapter 5

As the boys dismounted, Liberty asked, "Why are you staring at the portal like that? You look like you've seen a ghost."

I ignored Liberty as I concentrated on the portal. After a couple of seconds the swirling vortex starting shrinking until it disappeared altogether.

"That was close," I mumbled. I was worried Elizabeth would confront me upon my return to Manchester but for now we appeared to be safe.

"Get behind the building! Quick!" whispered Tommy, who grabbed my arm and pulled me back.

Tommy, Cam, and I had our backs against a two-story colonial building with a redbrick foundation and woodsiding. I looked up and saw a solid brick chimney with smoke that drifted up into sky. I quickly surveyed my surroundings. Even though the sun had just dipped below the neighboring frontier, it was plain to see that this wasn't

England. It was a rugged landscape. No trimmed hedges or courtyards. Instead, a grove of trees thick with underbrush created an eerie scene just in front of us. A barking dog could be heard in the distance.

"I saw a bunch of guys that looked like British soldiers," said Tommy. "I don't think they saw us."

I peeked around the corner of the building and saw about six British soldiers who were leaving the establishment. Their red coats made them easy to spot.

"No wonder the thirteen colonies won the war," said Liberty, who peered over my shoulder. "Those guys stand out like a cherry on an ice-cream sundae!"

As the soldiers marched away in unison I said, "Liberty, can you verify our location?"

"Yes, Captain! Seventeen sixty-five Virginia." He turned to Tommy and Cam and said, "I pay very close attention when Rush Revere announces our future historical destination. In fact, right now my time-travel senses tell me that Patrick Henry is very close by."

"Your time-travel senses?" Tommy asked.

"Yep!" Liberty nodded. "It's hard to explain."

"Is it like a tingling feeling at the base of your skull?" Tommy said, curiously.

Liberty looked surprised and said, "Actually, yes! How did you know?"

Tommy smiled, "It's the same kind of feeling that Spider-Man gets when he senses danger. His Spider-Sense gives him a psychological awareness of his surroundings. It sounds like your Time-Travel-Sense gives you a chronological sense of history as well as a keen awareness of the historical figure we're looking for."

"You mean I have a super power?" Liberty asked, like he just found out that school had been canceled. "Wow! I never thought of it like that. Wait, let me try using my super sense!" Liberty closed his eyes as if he were concentrating.

"Your horse, he really can talk!" said Cam. "And we really did jump through some kind of worm hole to the year 1765!" He laughed and added, "That's sick!"

"You're sick?" Liberty asked. "Maybe you have time-travel motion sickness, you know, like seasickness."

"Not sick like *ill*, he means sick like *awesome*!" Tommy clarified.

"That makes no sense at all," said Liberty. "I would not be feeling awesome if I were sick." Suddenly, Liberty was distracted by the sound of someone playing the fiddle. "Where is that music coming from?" he asked, listening more intently.

"I should probably set some ground rules," I said to Tommy and Cam. "I want us to be extra cautious since we've already seen British soldiers, okay? I don't expect any problems but you never know."

"It's like we're in a virtual world, isn't it?" asked Cam.

"Yes," I nodded, "except this is not a virtual world. Those Redcoats are real and their swords and bayonets and muskets are real too. So what I'm saying is no goofing off, got it?"

"Got it," said the boys in unison.

"All right," I said, "it looks like we're ready to . . . hey, where's Liberty?"

"He was here a second ago," Cam said.

I cautiously walked around the building to where the front doors were. Across the street was a larger building with a sign that was barely visible. It said Hanover County Courthouse. A few other buildings could be seen up and down the dimly lit street.

"Hey, there's Liberty," said Cam, pointing to the building we were hiding behind. "And it sounds like there's a party going on inside."

Liberty was standing near the front door and bobbing his head to the rhythm of the fiddle. I could also hear several voices talking and laughing from inside the establishment.

"What kind of building is this?" Tommy asked.

"My guess is a tavern," I said.

"You mean, like a bar?" Tommy asked.

"Yes," I confirmed. "No worries. There aren't any biker gangs in the eighteenth century."

Liberty walked back to where we were standing and sighed, "I guess this means I have to stay out here."

"We'll be back soon," I said. "In the meantime, we need you to keep a lookout for any Redcoats," I said.

"That is sort of important," Liberty said. "I've got you covered!"

I noticed Tommy pull something from his pocket. "Have some bubble gum," he said as he unwrapped the gum and tossed it to Liberty who snatched it out of the air with his lips.

"Oh, I've always wanted to try this," Liberty said as he chewed. "How exactly do you blow a bubble?"

Tommy smiled, maneuvered his own piece of gum in his mouth, and then began to blow.

"Fascinating!" said Liberty.

I rolled my eyes and said, "Let's enter the tavern."

As we entered we saw several tables against each wall. Well-dressed men with bright-colored coats and tricorn hats like the one I wore were sitting among the tables. Other men with collarless shirts and vests were seated as well and all the men were wearing breeches, stockings, and leather shoes. Candles flickered at each table as well as in sconces fixed to the walls. Men were telling stories, drinking from mugs, or playing cards. One man sat alone at an empty table playing the fiddle.

"Let's join the man with the fiddle," I suggested. "Perhaps he can tell us which of these men is Patrick Henry."

"Wait a second," said Cam. "Do you mean *the* Patrick Henry, as in one of America's Founding Fathers?"

"The very one," I confirmed.

"No way!" Cam beamed. "You know I'm a history buff, right? Patrick Henry is a rock star! Seriously, I've read his speeches and he was amazing! He's the guy who said, 'Give me liberty or give me death!'"

"That's right," I said. "He was one of the most influential champions of the American Revolution. Benjamin Franklin highly recommended that we visit him."

"Man, this is an awesome field trip. Thanks for inviting me!" Cam said.

As we approached the man with the fiddle he stopped playing. He wore a purple vest and linen shirt. His purple coat with gold buttons was thrown over a chair. He looked to be in his late twenties, maybe thirty years old. His hair was neatly combed and pulled back into a short ponytail.

"Excuse me, sir," I said, "but can you tell me which of these men is Patrick Henry?"

"Patrick Henry!" he exclaimed in an animated whisper. "You don't want to be associated with him. Haven't you heard? He's a radical! He's an outspoken lawyer that says what he will even if he offends the King!"

I was surprised by the man's warning and said, "Yes, well, we understand he's an opponent of the King's Stamp Act."

"Shh," said the man with the fiddle. "Don't speak so loudly when you talk about the Stamp Act that way. Do you want the King's spies to hear you?" The man glanced over our shoulders at the other men in the tavern. "Come, sit with me. You tell me what you've heard and I'll tell you what I've heard about that rabble-rouser Patrick Henry."

We each grabbed a chair and sat around the table. I glanced at the other men who were talking and laughing. Any one of them could be Henry, I supposed. Unless he wasn't here, but Liberty seemed so certain about it.

"Forgive my manners," said our new host. "You must be parched. What can I get you to drink?"

"You're too kind," I said. "I'd like some tea."

"And what would your servants care to drink?" He looked toward Tommy and Cam and said, "I assume these are your servants? Or perhaps one is your son and the other a slave, a well-dressed slave I must say." He glanced at Cam's dark skin and clothes.

Cam was clearly surprised by the comment, and his face contorted into an odd look of calm and consternation that I hadn't seen in him before. I put my hand on his shoulder and was about to say something reassuring but instead Cam boldly exclaimed, "I understand this is 1765 and you aren't enlightened to the reality of freedom for all men yet, but I am free and will always be free, just like this country."

I was impressed with his strength and composure in a difficult moment.

The fiddler smiled and looked thoroughly impressed with Cam. He said, "Well, I certainly do apologize, young man. I meant no offense."

Tommy looked relieved.

Suddenly, the fiddler jumped up onto his chair and with a foot on the table and his fiddle underneath his chin he began to play a fervent tune while tapping his foot. I looked at Tommy and Cam, who were all smiles. Tommy looked back at me and mouthed the words, *I think this guy is nuts!* Cam nodded with enthusiasm and gave me the universal symbol for crazy by twirling his finger near the side of his head. And just when I thought it couldn't get any stranger, the fiddler stopped playing and sprang with both feet on top of the wooden table. That's when he started singing and acting out his song!

Our worthy forefathers—let's give them a cheer—
To climates unknown did courageously steer;
Thro' oceans to deserts, for freedom they came,
And, dying, bequeath'd us their freedom and fame!

The room burst into applause and cheers. Some of the men were louder than others but all seemed to applaud the man's song. The men soon returned to their own conversations and the room became quiet, as it had been before.

The fiddler stepped down and patted Cam on the shoulder. "We shall all drink to freedom tonight," said the fiddler. "With whom do I have the pleasure of drinking?"

I replied, "This is Tommy and Cam, my apprentices. And my name is Rush Revere. I'm a history teacher and I was—"

"Revere, you say? Hmm, are you related to Paul Revere?"

"I believe I am!" I exclaimed. "I mean I've not actually met him but I'm a great admirer and we fight for the same cause."

"I'm glad to hear that," the man said, smiling. "Now then, perhaps Tommy and Cam would enjoy a cup of chocolate?"

"That's sounds great!" Tommy said. "Thank you!"

"Yeah," Cam said with a wink, "freedom and chocolate are definitely worth fighting for!"

The man laughed and waved at the barkeep, who walked over to our table and took our orders. When he left I asked, "Where do you think we could find Patrick Henry?"

"You'd be better off without him," the man sniffed. "I heard he just gave a speech at the House of Burgesses in Virginia's capital, Williamsburg. They say he spoke like thunder as he defended the rights of the colonies. He attacked the Stamp Act and said that the British Empire had no right to tax the American colonies. He said if we don't stop King George III now he'll keep taxing the people until he has us all in chains."

"I'm curious, what did the people say when they heard his speech?" I asked.

"Ha! The governor of Virginia was furious!" said the man, who picked up his fiddle, again. "Especially when Patrick Henry said the stamp tax was a threat to our liberty! That's when some of the older men cried, 'Treason!'" The man played a fast and gloomy tune on his fiddle. He stopped playing and continued. "People say Patrick Henry is verbally attacking the King! Would you believe he actually compared King George to Julius Caesar and Charles I."

"Wow, that's harsh," Cam said. "Julius Caesar was a Roman dictator and King Charles was beheaded for crimes against England. Sounds like Patrick Henry is really going out on a dangerous limb here. He's putting himself at risk."

"Perhaps your Patrick Henry values the cause of freedom more than his life," said the fiddler.

"That's why I like him so much," said Cam as he looked around the room. "I'd really like to meet him. I was hoping he could give me a few tips on how to speak like thunder! I'm thinking about running for student body president and speaking like thunder could come in handy." Cam stood up from his chair and mimicked his presidential speech, declaring, "Students of America! You say you want freedom to speak your mind. You say you want your voice to be heard! You say you want a leader who will defend your rights and extend your lunch hour. If you vote for me I promise liberty and justice for all!"

Liberty must have thought someone called his name because his head briefly appeared in the window and I saw him rigorously chewing his bubble gum. At least he wasn't getting into trouble.

As Cam sat down the fiddler stood up and began to applaud. In a booming voice, he said, "You have my vote! You are a most excellent orator, Cam. And you are brave to be so bold. Never let fear stop you from saying what needs to be said."

The barkeep of the tavern politely interrupted and set our beverages on the table. Wisps of steam rose from the silver mugs.

Tommy leaned over his mug and smelled the wafting aroma of chocolate. "Wow, that smells delicious!"

Cam sipped from his mug and said, "It's a little different than what we have back home! This is creamier and little bit sour."

"And where is *back home* for you?" asked the fiddler.

"We just moved from Colorado. My dad is in the military so we move every year or so. I guess I really don't have a place I call home," Cam replied.

"Colorado?" the man asked. "Is this a new settlement in the West? I've not heard of it."

Just then the door burst open and a young man about seventeen or eighteen burst into the tavern. The men on either side of the room turned to see who or what the ruckus was. The boy took off his tricorn hat and wiped his brow. He scanned the room quickly and then rushed over to our table and tossed several newspapers in front of our host.

"I brought the newspapers just like you asked, Mr. Henry," the boy panted. "The other messengers arrived just like you said they would, from Maryland and Rhode Island and Massachusetts and other colonies. They've all printed your seven resolutions against the Stamp Act. It looks like the colonies have united in opposing the stamp tax!"

"Henry?" I asked the boy. "Do you mean Patrick Henry?" I asked again, this time turning to the man with the fiddle.

Patrick Henry gave a big hearty laugh to match Cam's wide smile. "I'm afraid you're sitting with a treasonous radical who defies the King of England!" thundered Patrick with a giant grin.

I could hardly believe my ears. All this time we were sitting with one of the legendary forefathers of America! I blushed and said, "Forgive me, Mr. Henry. I should've recognized you earlier!"

"Recognized me?" asked Patrick. "Have we met before?"

I realized I couldn't tell him that his picture is in every American history book.

Patrick Henry proposes the Virginia Stamp Act
Resolutions to the House of Burgesses in Virginia.

"He means he should have recognized your voice of thunder," Cam joked.

Patrick laughed and said, "Cam, I enjoy your company." After a moment, he became more serious and exclaimed, "Now that you know who I am I want you to know something about me, something that has troubled me for years." He turned to look at Cam and said somberly, "The truth is I am very sorry to report that I own slaves."

"Why?" Cam asked, sincerely. "How can you say you're fighting for freedom and still own slaves? Isn't that hypocritical?"

"Slavery has become an important part of the economy here in the South," said Patrick. "But I have felt a great need to change the way things are in these southern colonies. Truly, I have felt tormented as my soul has wrestled with the owning of slaves, and I have come to realize that this wicked practice must come to an end. If we truly want to be a free people, a free land, a free America, then we must free the slaves. God cannot bless a country that allows the bondage and captivity of men, women, and children." He took a deep breath, sighed, and said, "Indeed, I believe a time will come when we shall abolish this lamentable evil called slavery."

Cam said, "That sounds like a very good start!" Then Cam raised his hand and said, "High five!" He prompted Patrick to raise his hand as well. Patrick slowly lifted his hand and Cam slapped his upraised palm.

Curious, Patrick asked, "You call that a *high five?*"

"Yeah," Cam replied. "It's a gesture of triumph or success. It also means we're friends."

"I like the high five," said Patrick.

"Wait until you learn the chest bump!" Tommy smiled.

Patrick noticed that the boy who had delivered the newspapers was watching with great curiosity about five feet away. Patrick flipped the boy a large silver coin and the boy caught it in the air.

"Thank you, Mr. Henry!" said the teenage boy, grinning from ear to ear. "If you will excuse me, sir, there is a peculiar horse out in the front of the tavern that caught my attention."

"Why did you say *peculiar* horse?" I asked nervously.

The boy replied with wonder, "In truth, this horse had a large pink bubble attached to his mouth. It was small at first but then it grew to the size of a cantaloupe until it finally popped. Then the horse used his tongue to lick up the pink sap that stuck to his nose and lips until it was all back in his mouth and he began chewing it. I'm hoping he'll do it again. I've never seen anything like it!"

"Cam and I will come with you," Tommy said. "I'm pretty sure I know what it is." The boys got up from the table, thanked Mr. Henry for the hot chocolate, and exited the tavern.

As Patrick Henry browsed the first newspaper I took out my phone, slipped it under the table, and typed a quick Facebook entry. *Virginia 1765. Sitting here drinking tea with Patrick Henry! Historians say that he was the man who sparked America's revolution. His seven resolutions to the Stamp Act articulated why America should reject and resist British taxation on the colonies. This brought on the Revolutionary War and finally separated America and England and gave independence to the colonies, which eventually became the United States of America!*

"Listen to this," said Patrick as he read from the newspaper he was holding. "This writer reports on my speeches and my opposition to the King and his Parliament. He writes, 'The tendons on Patrick Henry's neck stood out white and rigid like whipcords. His voice rose louder and louder, until the walls of the building seemed to shake. Men leaned forward in their seats, their faces pale.'" Patrick's laughter seemed to bounce off the walls. When he stopped he said, "They are scared of what the King will do when he finds out the colonies refuse to pay his stamp tax. What the King needs to understand is that before we will obey his laws we must have representation in Parliament. We want to help create the laws for the colonies. We demand the right to have our voices heard in England!"

I realized my jaw was open as I listened to Patrick Henry defend the colonies. I finally said, "I admire your fearlessness, speaking out against the King. But you realize if your words get back to England the King is bound to send his Redcoats after you for treason. This is serious. They may hang you!"

With a smile on his face and a steely gaze in his eyes he said, "If this be treason, make the most of it!"

As if on cue the door burst open again and Tommy stood in the doorway. Panicked, he said, "Mr. Revere! You better get out here. Cam's in trouble. The Redcoats are back and they've arrested him!"

Patrick and I sprang from the table and followed Tommy out of the tavern. It was nearly dark outside, and one of three British soldiers held a torch. Patrick was the first to reach the second soldier, who was nearest to Cam. His hands were cuffed and he shrugged when I looked at him. Tommy and the messenger boy were watching close by.

"What's the meaning of this?" shouted Patrick. His voice did sound like thunder and the second soldier took a step back.

Feeling threatened, the third soldier unsheathed his sword and held it in front of him. The first soldier did the same.

"It was an accident," Cam said, defending himself.

Tommy leaned close to me and whispered, "Liberty was tired of chewing his gum so Cam told him to spit it out and I sort of dared him to try and hit one of the soldiers as they walked by the tavern. The soldier was at least twenty yards away. I didn't think he'd actually do it!"

The second soldier, who must have put the cuffs on Cam, stepped forward and said, "Your slave threw a wad of pink sap and hit me in the side of the head." The soldier turned and, sure enough, a sticky mass of gum looked like it had been pulled from his hair, but it was still a gooey mess.

"He's not a slave!" shouted Tommy.

"Shut up, colonial dog!" yelled one of the soldiers. Before Tommy could react the soldier closest to him swung the butt of his gun into Tommy's head and knocked him down.

"Enough of this!" I screamed as I rushed over to make sure Tommy wasn't hurt. Tommy pulled his hand away from where the gun had hit his head and found blood on his fingers. I quickly examined the cut and said, "It's not bad. It barely broke the skin. But you're going to have a goose egg on the side of your head." I looked up and saw Patrick ready to make his move. He remained calm, but I could tell he was also worried about Tommy and nervous for his young friend, Cam.

Cam nervously laughed and said, "I didn't throw it!" His eyes darted toward Liberty, who was doing an excellent job at pretending to be just a horse. Cam firmly said, "You didn't see me throw it. You didn't see any of us throw it! I have rights! Where's a lawyer when I need one?"

"I am a lawyer!" said Patrick Henry. He walked closer to the soldier near Cam but the two soldiers with swords stood firm.

Hearing the shouts and yells, the men from the tavern came outside to see Tommy bleeding and Cam in cuffs. Their expressions turned from concern for the young boys to anger at the soldiers.

Patrick shouted, "England will always consider us inferior! I have seen the way you Lobsterbacks laugh at how we talk and the way we dress. You have forgotten that we are still British subjects. Now, you believe we are dim-witted farmers and ill-suited merchants. You would sooner keep us in a barn then invite us into your chambers as equals."

"You will never be our equals, colonial scum," said the soldier in the middle. "Now get out of our way before we lock you up with the slave. You are no better than filthy rats! We should lock up the whole lot of you and let you rot in chains."

The men from the tavern started murmuring and cursing the soldiers. These were blacksmiths and carpenters and farmers—men with burly arms and itching to fight. The Redcoats knew they were outnumbered but they stood their ground.

The soldier holding a torch in one hand and his sword in the other sneered at Patrick and said, "We are taking our prisoner and he will be judged according to his crimes. Now get out of the way!"

Cam's jaw dropped in desperation and he said, "Uh-oh. Guys? Help me. Somebody?"

Patrick Henry looked as determined as ever and bellowed, "Crimes? You dare speak of crimes? I will tell you who the criminals are. The men who sit in Parliament and a king who burdens his people with unfair taxes."

"Your words convict you of treason!" said the first soldier. "You could hang for that!"

"As I've said before, if this be treason, make the most it!" said Patrick. "I spit on your stamp tax!" Patrick spit to the right.

"You are lucky to be walking freely in these streets," said the first solider. "We have direct orders from the King to put you in jail for any disrespect to the Crown."

"The King is the one disrespecting our freedom!" said Patrick, taking a step closer. "How dare he demand that we open our homes to house Redcoats like you! You are not our guests! You don't even like the people of these colonies. You just want to keep control of us. We worked hard to build these colonies. How dare the King force us to take you into our homes! This law is absurd! I spit on what the King is calling the Quartering Act!" Patrick spit again. "You Redcoats will not step foot inside of *my* home!"

"Watch your tongue, Patriot, before we cut it out," said the third soldier, who now pointed his sword directly at Patrick Henry.

But Patrick did not back down. He turned to the men from the tavern and shouted, "If we do not oppose the Quartering Act, the Redcoats will soon be tossing your families from their bedchambers in order to move in! Your wives and your children will be out in the streets and all because the King is an oppressive, arrogant, and selfish tyrant who only cares about three things: taxes, taxes, and more taxes!"

The colonists behind us shouted and jeered at the injustice in front of them. "Let them go!" said a large colonist with the neck the size of Rhode Island.

And that's when I noticed Liberty behind the soldier with the torch. While Patrick Henry was speaking he must have slipped behind unnoticed. Before the soldiers could react, Liberty turned his hind legs toward his target and gently kicked the unsuspecting soldier in the rear end. Even a gentle kick sent the Redcoat four feet into the air. He landed with a thud in front of us, his torch and sword rolling to our feet. I took the torch and Tommy took the sword. As if to prove a point, the third soldier raised his sword and attempted to strike down Patrick. The blade was deflected as Tommy parried with his own sword. Again and again the two swords clashed and remarkably it looked like Tommy had the upper hand. As the soldier stumbled backward, Liberty conveniently tripped him and the soldier fell to the ground. The colonists cheered at the momentary victory and pressed forward against the three Redcoats, who quickly retreated, leaving Cam standing alone and handcuffed.

"It would be wise for us all to leave this place for a time," said Patrick as the men dispersed from the tavern. "We can expect more Redcoats and they will want revenge. Do you have a place to go?"

"Yes, we'll be safe," I said. "And thank you for your help today."

"No kidding," said Cam. "You basically saved my life!"

"I try to save at least one life a day." Patrick winked. "Lucky for you, I had not yet filled my quota!"

We all laughed and Patrick finally said, "Cam, you are a remarkable young man. It took me a long time to have the confidence to stand up for what I wanted to do, who I wanted to be. But I have found that I am happiest when I am defending freedom and helping others find liberty and justice."

"Me, too!" said Cam. "When I was younger I was a military

brat. My family had just moved to a new city, and it's never easy starting over at a new school. And to make it worse, I was this little runt of a kid. These bigger kids at my old school used to bully me. They did some really mean things. One time they tossed me into a trash can upside down. But one summer I had a huge growth spurt. I grew seven inches and gained almost ten pounds. That's the year I decided to act and not be acted upon. So now whenever I see someone being bullied I don't stand for it. I can't help it. I like defending the little guy. I like helping others find liberty and justice, too!"

Patrick smiled and said, "The truth is you remind me of me when I was younger. You have a gift for words, a clever mind, and a sense of humor. No wonder I feel like we are kindred spirits." He reached out to shake Cam's hand but the handcuffs made it awkward.

Cam laughed, "Oops, forgot about the cuffs."

Patrick smiled and gently placed his hand on Cam's shoulder. He looked Cam straight in the eyes and said, "And I will not forget about the evils of slavery, I promise. As God is my witness, I will give my life for the cause of freedom for all men."

"Goodbye, Mr. Henry," said Tommy.

"Goodbye, Tommy," Patrick said, beaming. "You are quite the swordsman."

"I had a good teacher," said Tommy. With all the practice he had with Myles Standish, the Pilgrims' military leader, it's no surprise that he fought like he did. Myles would be proud!

"Safe travels, Rush Revere," said Patrick. "Until we meet again!" He turned to enter the tavern for his fiddle and coat.

I turned back to Tommy, Cam, and Liberty, and said, "That was quite the adventure! But I'm ready to return to modern-day."

"Me, too!" they all said in unison.

As we walked to the back of the tavern, I took a deep breath and said, "There's a chance we'll run into Elizabeth when we return to the school."

"Why do you say that?" Tommy asked.

"Because when we time-jumped to visit Patrick Henry she was chasing after us and nearly jumped through the time portal before it closed."

"What!" Tommy exclaimed.

"Hey! Maybe we can get Elizabeth to shoot laser beams out of her eyes," said Liberty.

"How is that going to help us?" complained Tommy.

"Well, somebody's got to get those handcuffs off Cam," said Liberty.

"Now we're talking," Cam said with a chuckle. "But laser beams really aren't my first choice."

"No worries," I told him as I reached into Liberty's saddlebag in search of a solution to Cam's dilemma. "Ah, here it is!"

"That is one odd-looking key," Cam said.

"It's a skeleton key and it can pick any eighteenth-century lock." I inserted the key into the lock of Cam's handcuffs and presto!

"I can't tell you how good it feels to be free!" exclaimed Cam.

I nodded and said, "It's a great feeling, isn't it. Likewise, the laws and taxes that the King and Parliament keep mandating to the colonies are like handcuffs. They restrict and bind the colonists from living and growing and being a free America!"

"Never thought of it like that. We're going to need a much bigger key to unlock that problem," Cam said.

"No kidding," Tommy agreed. "I think it's called a revolution!"

Tommy and Cam lifted themselves up onto Liberty's saddle.

"Now, about Elizabeth. We need to return to someplace different than where we left."

"Hmm," said Liberty. "How about in the hallway in front of our classroom. We've done that before."

"Can your Time-Travel-Sense tell us if anyone is in the hallway?" Cam asked.

"It's worked before," Liberty said. "I mean, I'm still trying to figure all of this out, but I think I can do it so no one sees us."

"Okay, then let's go," I said. "Tommy, how's the cut on your head?"

"It feels like a linebacker hit me without my football helmet on," Tommy said with a smile. "Besides that, I'm good."

I sighed, relieved that we were leaving without further harm. "That was a tough one for all us," I said. "I'm just glad you're both okay. Liberty, take us home!"

"*Rush, rush, rushing from history,*" Liberty said.

In the dark of the night, the time portal opened again and as we headed toward the swirling, circular light I readied myself for whatever was waiting for us on the other side.

Wouldn't you be scared to have soldiers force their way into your home?

Chapter 6

The fluorescent lights in the school hallway made me squint as we returned to the twenty-first century. Once again, Liberty hit the bull's-eye as we landed in front of our classroom door. I quickly surveyed the scene and noticed we were alone.

Relieved, I said, "Nice jumping, Liberty. You boys need to change your clothes and—"

Just then I heard a single pair of footsteps running down the connecting hallway. The footsteps were getting louder. I assumed we returned just seconds after we had left, just seconds after Elizabeth had seen us jump through the time portal. I was certain those were her footsteps racing back to my classroom to prove I was a neglectful and delinquent teacher. The footsteps sounded like they would turn the corner any second and Elizabeth would find us! I desperately called to Liberty, who was already disappearing, but the boys were still sitting on top of, well, nothing!

"Oops," said Tommy. "I thought we'd turn invisible with Liberty if we were sitting on top of him." Still five feet off the ground, they quickly kicked their legs over to one side and slipped off an invisible saddle.

Freedom stood there and smiled. "Real slick, guys," she said nearly laughing. "You're lucky it's just me."

"Why were you running down the hallway like that?" I asked.

"When my grandfather dropped me off in front of the school I sprinted to the classroom hoping I could still catch you before you time-jumped. But by the look of things I'm guessing you just returned."

"It was incredible!" said Cam like he had just come off a wild roller coaster. "We traveled to the year 1765 and met Patrick Henry!"

"And I learned how to blow a bubble with bubble gum!" said Liberty.

"I thought you were going to be at the dentist today?" asked Tommy, apologetically. "You told me you wouldn't be back until almost the end of class."

Freedom shrugged her shoulders and said, "No cavities."

"You're lucky," Cam said. "The worst part is when the dentist has to numb your gums. I mean, I'm glad for the anesthesia. It's the shot I don't like."

"Anesthesia, spelled A-N-E-S-T-H-E-S-I-A," said Liberty, proudly. "Now, give Tommy a word and see if he can spell it. We're having a spelling bee competition. Unless Tommy is scared," Liberty taunted. "Of course, he shouldn't feel bad losing to a horse since technically I'm no ordinary horse although I look ordinary but most people who do extraordinary things appear ordinary at first until the moment that they—"

"Thanks, Liberty," Freedom said with a smirk. "You just gave me an idea. Tommy, spell the word *logorrhea*."

"Huh?" Tommy said while raising one eyebrow.

Liberty smiled and said, "I don't know what the word means but I approve of your word choice."

Tommy took off his hat and scratched his head. "Um, can you give it to me in a sentence?"

"Sure," said Freedom. "Liberty's logorrhea can go on and on but it's one of the things I like about him."

"Oh, I think I know," Tommy said, smiling. "*Logorrhea* is spelled L-O-G-O-R-R-H-E-A."

"Correct," Freedom said.

"Wait a minute," said Liberty suspiciously. "Are you saying that I . . ."

"That you have a big mouth and talk too much? Yes!" said Elizabeth, who appeared from behind the hallway corner. She wore a long red coat with designer jeans and a matching red headband in her hair. "My, my, my, what do we have here?" Elizabeth slowly walked in between us with her hands behind her back. She stared at each of us and talked as if she knew a secret. "Do any of you have hall passes? No, I'm sure you don't because that would require one of you to have a responsible teacher." She glared at me and then looked away. "Do any of you have any fashion sense at all?" She stopped in front of Freedom with a look of disdain. "Freedom? Or should I just call you Free-*dumb*! That's spelled D-U-M-B. By the way, you looked better in that hideous Pilgrim costume that should've been burned in the seventeenth century." She released her gaze and finally approached Liberty. "Oh, and finally, do any you have a permit for this"—she scrunched up her nose in disgust—"this odoriferous horse inside Manchester Middle School?"

"Odoriferous?" said Liberty. "For the record, I'm hardly offended by your weak insults."

"Oh, that wasn't an insult," Elizabeth said. "That was simply a fact. I'm sure you know that *odoriferous* means smelly. Personally, I don't like the smell of horses. It's a foul stench that belongs in a barn, not a school." Elizabeth turned to look at all of us and said, "I'm on to your little secret. I saw you jump through that magical door thingy. It's a time portal, isn't it?" I must've looked surprised because she said, "I knew it! And don't look so surprised. It's obvious with all the colonial costumes and the movie you showed us about the Pilgrims in Holland and the talking horse who knows about American history."

"Just what is it you're going to do, Elizabeth?" I asked.

"What am I going to do?" she asked, acting surprised. "It's not about what *I'm* going to do. It's about what *you're* going to do for *me*."

"That sounds like blackmail," said Cam.

"At least one of you has some brains," Elizabeth scoffed.

"Whatever," Tommy said. "We'll all deny what you've seen and heard and you'll end up with the nurse again."

"Already thought of that," said Elizabeth. "That's why I had the custodian help me install that small camera in the corner of the ceiling." We followed her gaze and saw the lens pointing right at us. "So let's get this straight. Either you do what I say or I take the video to my daddy and it's bye-bye Mr. Revere. No more Liberty. And I'm pretty sure I can get the rest of you expelled from Manchester Middle School."

"Why are you so mean?" asked Freedom.

Elizabeth sighed and said, "Freedom, I'm not mean. I'm simply taking control of the situation. You see, when things get out of control I have to tighten the controls. Let me put it this way. Some people were meant to rule, that's me, and other people are meant to be ruled, that's you. Some people are superior, that's me. And some people are inferior, that's you."

"Mr. Revere," called Tommy, "I say we take Elizabeth with us the next time we time travel. Seriously, I know just the person she should meet. I bet she's a direct descendant."

I knew exactly whom Tommy was thinking of.

"I knew Thomas would get it," said Elizabeth.

"My name's Tommy," he said.

Elizabeth sighed, "Tommy is a child's name. Thomas is much more sophisticated. Plus, Thomas and Elizabeth sound much better together, don't you think?"

"Excuse me?" asked Tommy with a stunned look on his face.

"I've been thinking since you're the star quarterback and I'm the most popular girl in school that we'd be perfect as the homecoming king and queen. Then we can rule the school together," Elizabeth said, smiling, "just as long as you do exactly what I say."

Cam nearly laughed out loud and Freedom just rolled her eyes.

"I don't know what warped fantasy world you're living in," Tommy replied, "but keep me out of it."

Elizabeth ignored Tommy's remark and impatiently said, "The day isn't getting any younger, people. I want to time-travel now."

"Now?" Tommy asked, surprised.

Liberty looked heartbroken. "But I thought it was time for me to finally perform for the class my stomp act about the Stamp Act!" he whined.

"If she's time-traveling, then count me out," said Freedom, crossing her arms.

"Me, too," said Cam.

"Me, three," Tommy said.

Elizabeth grabbed Tommy's arm and said, "I insist that Thomas travel with me. Riding behind him will be the only thing that gets me on that horse."

"Oh brother," Tommy mumbled.

Elizabeth continued: "And another thing: I'm not wearing any colonial clothing. It makes you look like orphans. Except for you, Mr. Revere. You look like you should be in an insane asylum."

This girl was starting to get on my nerves. I took a deep breath and exhaled slowly. She would have to wear the appropriate clothing if she wanted to time-travel but I'd deal with that later. I sighed and said, "Very well, Elizabeth, if time-traveling is what you want, time-traveling is what you'll get. But for the record, you're not forcing me to do anything. I'm happy to take you and teach you what only history can share. But mark my words, history has a way of showing us the good, the bad, and the ugly. Are you prepared for that?"

Elizabeth simply shook her head and rolled her eyes. "Mr. Revere," she said, "I deal with the good, the bad, and the ugly every day at Manchester Middle School. For example, my fashion sense is the *good*. And Freedom's fashion sense is the *bad* and the *ugly*."

"I'm outta here," Freedom said, giving one last glare to Elizabeth. "Bye, guys, I'm going to class." As she walked toward the classroom door she turned back and looked at Liberty. I suspected she was sending him a telepathic message.

Liberty whinnied and smiled. He whispered, "Freedom thinks we should take Elizabeth to the past and leave her there."

"I'm outta here, too," said Cam. "I better change my clothes before all the girls see me. That's right, I've seen Elizabeth like she's all desperate to know how I make these colonial clothes look so good! We can hang later, Lizzy," Cam winked.

"My name is Elizabeth, you moron."

"Whatever," Cam said, casually. "Maybe I'll see you guys at the football game tomorrow night." Cam gave us a giant smile and strutted toward the bathroom.

I turned to Elizabeth and said, "Are you sure I can't persuade you to wear something more appropriate for our eighteenth-century visit?"

Elizabeth sighed as if she felt sorry for me. She replied, "I should be asking you the same question." And then in a very condescending tone she began pointing to what she was wearing and slowly said, "*This* is a Le Pluer jacket and *these* are Yass jeans and my Pomanelli shoes are from *It-al-y*. You, on the other hand, are wearing scraps and rags from the thrift store. I'm surprised you're not pushing a shopping cart with all your belongings in-side."

My mouth dropped open slightly in disbelief. Did she just call me a hobo?

Tommy replied, "Elizabeth, you can't show up like that and not expect people to start asking questions . . ."

As he continued to try to explain the potential danger of a girl wearing jeans in the eighteenth century, I turned to Liberty and whispered an idea into his ear.

Liberty mused, "Hmm, yes, that might be the perfect solu-tion."

"Good," I whispered, "and I still have Freedom's colonial dress;

that should fit Elizabeth." I interrupted Tommy and Elizabeth and said, "It's time we show Elizabeth what time-jumping is all about."

Tommy lifted himself up onto Liberty's saddle and I helped up Elizabeth, who sat right behind him.

"Liberty, it's time we visit Windsor Castle in England. It seems like a place that would suit Elizabeth."

"Windsor Castle is a part of American history?" Tommy asked.

"It's the residence of King George III," I said. "And he was very involved in shaping American history."

"Meeting a king sounds great but what are we waiting for?" asked Elizabeth sounding irritated. "Enough chitchat. Sitting on top of your donkey is making me gag. Seriously, the smell is like a manure pile. Let's go already!"

"Some people need a swift kick in the you-know-where," Liberty snorted.

"Let's just stick with our plan," I reassured him.

"Fine!" said Liberty. "It'll be my pleasure." He took a deep breath and firmly said, *"Rush, rush, rushing to history!"*

As the gold and purple time portal started to open, I hoped our plan would work. I ran closely behind Liberty as he galloped toward the portal. I shouted, "England, Windsor Castle, 1766, King George III."

As Liberty jumped I heard Elizabeth scream as she passed through the portal. I immediately followed and in the time it takes to hurdle a small fence I landed on the other side. The first thing I saw was Elizabeth sailing over Liberty's head and landing face-first in the middle of a small pond with several lily pads floating on the surface of the water.

Windsor Castle, Berkshire, the royal residence in England.

Tommy quickly jumped off Liberty and raced over to the edge of the shallow pond and yelled, "Elizabeth, are you okay? Let me help you out!"

Elizabeth pushed herself up, sopping wet. Her red headband was floating in the water and in its place was a limp lily pad. Her jacket and jeans were muddy and her mascara was smeared. As she slowly walked to the lawn that surrounded the pond I noticed she was missing one shoe. I could barely see it stuck in the mud about two feet under the water. Her hair was matted to her face, and although her mouth was open I wasn't sure if she was breathing.

Finally, the silence was broken when she screamed, "Ahhh! What. Just. Happened! What kind of horse stops like that! Are you kidding me?!"

Liberty confessed: "Um, well, I really didn't think you'd fall face-first into a pond. Sorry about that. The plan was to get your clothes a little muddy so you'd want to change them and wear something from the eighteenth century."

"I'm the one that makes the plans around here, remember!" Elizabeth shouted. "Ugh, just help me get out of this sewer! It smells putrid, almost as bad as Liberty."

Liberty ignored the insult, distracted by the new scenery. With wonder in his voice, he said, "Now that is a castle!"

Directly in front of us was a tall, massive, round stone tower. It was ancient-looking but matched all the smaller castle-like towers and buildings that surrounded us. The smaller towers were connected by a large stone wall that was clearly meant to keep out the unwanted. After a moment, I realized we were inside the grounds of Windsor Castle. The yard was beautifully landscaped with a variety of trees, shrubs, and flowers. The aroma from many varieties of roses was intoxicating. Birds chirped from the trees as bees buzzed around the garden. The scene was a paradise and very different from what the colonists were dealing with in a new country.

As Tommy helped Elizabeth to a small stone bench just a few yards away, I reached for my travel bag that had the colonial dress.

Suddenly, a voice from behind us yelled, "You there! What is your business?"

I turned to see three British soldiers running in our direction. Their red-coat uniforms looked brand-new. Their black boots shined and their gold buttons sparkled. Even their muskets looked polished, as if they had never been used. Life behind castle walls was certainly much different than life in the American wilderness, where British troops had to try to control headstrong colonists every day.

"How did you get into the castle?" asked the lead soldier. He sounded very annoyed.

"Would you believe we dropped out of the sky?" I said, jokingly. Apparently, my joke wasn't very funny, as the soldiers just glared at me. "As a matter of fact we have urgent news for the King," I said.

"Only those invited get to see the King," said the soldier, briskly. "Do you have an invitation?"

I paused for just a moment before Tommy butted in and lied: "We did but it's probably at the bottom of the pond. As you can see we had a little accident."

I smiled and said, "Yes, that's right. Poor girl. And now's she's

A portrait of George III, King of Great Britain and Ireland (1760–1820).

wet and freezing and I'm sure the King would not want any harm to come to one of his invited guests, especially one so young and beautiful."

Elizabeth just sat there looking cold and miserable.

The soldier looked at Elizabeth and then back to me. He paused before he finally said, "Very well. Follow me. But if the King is not expecting you—"

I interrupted and said, "I assure you the King will be glad we have arrived. Our news is of the utmost importance."

Soon we were following the lead soldier, with the other two soldiers following us. We approached a very large door big enough for Liberty to fit through. Two more Redcoats stood guard on either side of the door. We quickly entered into an immense hallway with colorful tapestries that hung from the stone walls. On one side of the hallway were full suits of armor from the Middle Ages. The armor stood like sentinels ready to come to life and protect the castle if need be. When we were halfway down the hallway we saw a tall man descend a stone stairway. The man was in his mid to late twenties. He looked young but was dressed in clothing worthy of a king. Everything he wore looked expensive and new. The rich colors of his clothes, his perfect posture, and even his powdered face intimidated me. The vision of this man was so royal, so majestic that I could barely speak.

As he reached the last step of the stairway I forced my tongue to comply with my mind and while bowing low I said, "King George, Your Excellency." Liberty bowed as well, which seemed to amuse the King. "I am Rush Revere, history teacher and historian. And these are my students, Tommy and Elizabeth. We've come to bring you news from the New World."

"Your Highness," the lead soldier said with a bow, "they insisted that their news was urgent."

The King looked me up and down as if to say *what are these peasants doing in my presence?* His eyes turned to Elizabeth and said, "Elizabeth is a fine name, a royal name. But why is she drenched from head to toe? Guard, find the maids and have them dress her in something appropriate. Take her to the Red Drawing Room when she is fit for company. And you can burn those rags she's wearing."

Elizabeth was staring at King George III as if he were a rock star. Surprisingly, she did not complain about her clothes getting burned. In fact, I wondered if she had heard him at all. Instead, she bowed low and said, "Thank you, Your Majesty. Your clothes are magnificent. You shine like gold. It's been a long journey but I am honored to be in your presence."

I was shocked by Elizabeth's sudden change in character. She was actually being nice and extremely polite! She played along perfectly and curtseyed to the King and then followed the guard while leaving a trail of water still dripping from her clothing.

"Is that the same girl we know? That's what you call sucking up!" whispered Tommy with a grin.

"Is something amusing?" King George asked, reminding us quickly of our surroundings.

"No, Your Excellency, quite the opposite," I said standing up straight. "There is a serious situation happening in the colonies."

"Let us retire to the Red Drawing Room. Guard, take Mr. Revere's horse to the livery."

It didn't take us long before we entered a magnificent room adorned with red velvet chairs with golden armrests. Huge golden-framed paintings of kings and queens lined the red fabric walls. The ceiling looked like it was painted with real gold leaf. Golden tables with intricate and expensive-looking vases and statues and golden clocks reminded me that we were indeed in a real castle with a real king and his real riches! Several of the King's guards entered the room with us.

"Tell me this important news from the colonies," said the King as he gracefully sat in a royal-looking chair and crossed his legs.

The king didn't smile but he wasn't frowning, either. Tommy and I found chairs and sat down. I said, "We are here to tell you that the people are not happy in America."

The King looked mildly interested in what I was saying but not very concerned. "What concern is that of mine?" he asked.

I was thrown off a bit by his question. I had expected him to ask me to explain further. Tommy looked at me with his eyebrows raised as if to say, what now?

I knew I couldn't change history, and I hadn't come to pick a fight. But I was determined to explain the colonial situation and, hopefully, learn some historical truth in the process. I said, "This should concern Your Majesty because the people are getting more and more angry. They left England for a reason. They were looking for freedom and the chance to really succeed with their lives."

"You came all this way to tell me that the colonists are fighting with the motherland? You think this is important information for me? You are a foolish man!" said the King in a raised voice.

I must say that his insult got under my skin. I respected that he is a king but I was born an American, and I wasn't thrilled about getting treated this way! I held my temper enough to say,

"Your Excellency, please if you would—you are mistreating the people, the taxes are too severe, and they cannot vote! This isn't the way to lead."

"Revere, I should throw you out in the moat this minute for your ridiculous statements. How dare you tell me how to be a leader! I am the head of England; I know exactly what I'm doing. The New World is our land and the people are ours. They must share their wealth with the homeland, they must pay taxes to England, and they must obey the wishes of the King!"

The guards in the room moved closer to King George as if I was some kind of threat.

Normally, I'm as cool as a cucumber, but this was getting out of control. The King was really laying into me now and I must say it was getting to me.

Tommy whispered, "No wonder Elizabeth is a fan! He's a bigger diva than she is!"

"Your Excellency, you are a smart man," I said. "Why are you pursuing this path? What benefit is there to Britain?" I was trying to remain detached as best I could, an observer of history.

"I do not need you to tell me I am smart! I do not need you to tell me anything, you buffoon!" the King said, pounding the bottom of his fist on his knee.

"With all due respect, Your Highness, I'm hardly a buffoon." I tried to maintain some sense of relaxed scholarship, but I was starting to sweat and my heart was starting to beat faster. I was either scared or angry or both! I continued: "I am just trying to figure out why you are so dedicated to limiting the rights of the Americans. Why do you treat them this way? Why are you taxing them so much?"

The King squinted at me and asked, "Do all the colonists

dress like you?" Before I could respond the King replied, "The hat you wear, it is atrocious. Your coat is that of a commoner. Your shoes look pale and unpolished. And your speech sounds ghastly. Do you have a speech impediment or was your mother simply as dumb as you are?"

Did he really just insult my mother? This king was pompous, rude, and inconsiderate. Frankly, he was a jerk!

"No matter, I will answer your insidious question," the King said. "The colonies are behaving like children. They have forgotten their mother country and for that they must be disciplined. They are not their own land or their own people! They are part of this country! They are under my rule and always will be!"

I knew I shouldn't provoke the King and was doubtful that anything I could say would get through to him. But he did insult my mother! I finally said, "Yes, children can be very rude. In fact, you, yourself, look very young. Was it you who chose to punish the colonists by creating the Stamp Act and Quartering Act?" My comment seemed to strike a nerve in the king.

"How dare you!" shouted the King.

The King's guards pressed forward and unsheathed their swords. King George raised his hand and the soldiers stopped. I imagine they thought my words had sentenced me to the dungeon. I doubt many people, if any, dared speak to the King of England like I had.

King George eased back in his chair and coldly said, "Parliament creates the rules based on what they feel is best for the colonies and best for England. The thirteen colonies need order. They need England like a baby needs its mother's milk." When he finished speaking he smirked with satisfaction.

I forced myself to remain calm and replied, "That is a good

point, Your Highness. But the colonies believe they are no longer babies. In fact, they believe they are no longer children. Their economy is thriving, their businesses are successful, and they refuse to be told what taxes they have to pay—"

The King interrupted and exclaimed, "And that is something that a child would say. I will have the colonies back under my control. These so-called Patriots will never succeed as individuals. They will bow to the King and serve the Crown. They will do what they are told. I will not tolerate anything less!"

"I'm not so sure about that," I whispered to Tommy. "The United States of America is going to be born soon."

Tommy whispered back, "This is better than Monday Night Football! Revere versus the King of England!" I was glad Tommy could have a sense of humor. The tension in the room was so thick you could slice it with a butter knife.

"You have some nerve, Revere! You took a great risk coming here and addressing me with this drivel!" The King's face was red and his eyes were fiercely focused on mine.

Whether good or bad, something inside me pushed onward. I could tell I was losing some of the history teacher and getting involved a little too much in the actual history. *Careful*, I said to myself. *Careful!*

"Your Excellency," I said, "what the people want is a vote. Why is that so hard to understand?"

"I recommended ending the stamp tax! Isn't that enough for you fools? You truly are children! I don't care what the colonists want!" the King yelled as he stood up from his chair. "I have heard from the provincial Benjamin Franklin. He is a fool to side with those who fight against the Crown. And rebels like Patrick Henry and Samuel Adams will hang from the gallows for their

treacherous words. I will have my way!" He pouted. "I will. I will! The colonists are rabble-rousers and common criminals. They are dumb, silly dressed fools who are still subject to my laws and my word. I shall not have them forget that I rule the New World. I am the King! The land and the people of the thirteen colonies are still mine. Mine, I tell you! The colonists will do anything I say and buy anything we sell them! Except for fine fashion, it appears!"

The King sneered with a wicked grin. "As a matter of fact, I am signing the Declaratory Act in the morning, which gives England and the King full authority, full power to make laws that are legally binding on the colonies."

"In other words," I said, "England's grip on America becomes even tighter."

"Like handcuffs?" asked Tommy.

"Exactly," I said. I stood and motioned for Tommy to stand as well. I tried to remain humble, realizing at any moment the King could tell the guards, Off with my head!

I took a deep breath and said, "This act, this Declaratory Act, will make my countrymen even angrier. It will feel like the freedoms their ancestors fought for are being taken away."

The King sneered and said, "You imbecile! The colonists have no idea what is best for them. They are not capable of making decisions for themselves. I am their king, and I know better than they do what is good for them! I want them totally dependent on me for everything. That is the way it always has been, that is the way it should be."

"I couldn't agree with you more Your Highness," said Elizabeth, who stood at the door of the Red Drawing Room. She was wearing the most exquisite blue gown, which seemed to sparkle.

George III, King of Great Britain and Ireland (1760–1820).

It reached all the way to the floor and looked like something from Cinderella's ball. A short white fur was draped across her shoulders and her hair was curled and beautifully arranged on top of her head. I could tell her face was powdered and she looked several years older than she really was.

"Elizabeth?" Tommy asked. "What the . . . did you bump your head when you fell into that pond?"

"The King is so wise and so amazingly handsome," Elizabeth said, ignoring Tommy. "I absolutely agree that taking control of the situation is the only thing to do. We need to do what needs to be done to help them see that the King's laws are just. We need the colonies to show more respect to England. We need to force them to obey! I declare that we put troops in every house and tax all the little fools!"

"We?" said Tommy. "And who made you queen? Maybe bringing you here wasn't such a good idea."

The King turned to Elizabeth and said, "It is reassuring to see this kind of transformation and hear this kind of loyalty from one of my colonial subjects."

"The point is a good leader is supposed to protect and preserve the rights of the people. Instead it appears as though you are trampling those rights with tyranny," I said, knowing full well I would break what little harmony there was in the room.

"I am done with you!" screamed King George. "I rule! And I grow tired of your insults." He walked toward Elizabeth, took her hand, and kissed it. "Elizabeth, I am glad for your company and wish we could have spent more time together." He then turned toward Tommy and me and shouted, "Guards! Escort my lady and the two bloody Americans to the front gate. Retrieve their horse from the livery and send them on their way."

Two guards escorted Elizabeth by the arms and another two escorted Tommy. As they left the room, King George called to me one last time. I was really not interested to hear what the King was about to say. In fact, I knew I had pushed the King too far and had overstayed my welcome.

That wicked grin returned to the King's lips and he said threateningly, "Mr. Revere, do not ever forget that I am king of the most powerful nation in the world. My word is law. Your pathetic life has been spared for one reason. I want you to sail back to your woeful America and tell those wretched rebels that I will send the entire British army to force them into submission if I have to. Do you understand? Or is that too difficult for your pea-sized brain."

"Oh, I understand," I said with a smirk. "It will be my pleasure."

Chapter 7

*A*fter *leaving the* castle we found a secluded area in a nearby forest to time-jump back to modern-day. Liberty suggested that I put duct tape over Elizabeth's mouth so we wouldn't have to hear her incessant complaining about getting kicked out of Windsor Castle.

"*Rush, rush, rushing from history,*" Liberty said.

Like clockwork, we arrived back at Manchester in the same hallway just seconds after we had left. In fact, Cam must have just finished changing into his modern-day clothes and was walking back to the classroom when he noticed us in the hallway.

"Haven't you guys left yet?" Cam asked. "What's taking you so . . ." That's when he noticed the dress that Elizabeth was wearing. "What happened to her?"

"Would you believe she fell into a pond?" Liberty said.

"More like thrown into a pond," Elizabeth countered.

"A pond?" asked Cam. "Was there a toad in the pond that kissed her and she turned into a princess?"

"I wouldn't let a toad kiss me! Gross! If we were in England I'd have the guards throw you into the dungeon!" Elizabeth said.

"She may look like a princess but she's acting like a toad," Cam replied.

"Let's get back into the classroom. I imagine the video of Benjamin Franklin is almost over," I said.

"Quick, someone take a picture of me wearing this dress!" said Elizabeth as she handed Tommy her phone. "It's the least you can do after ruining my visit with King George!" Tommy took a quick picture and handed the phone back to Elizabeth.

"I can't wait to post this on Facebook and Pinterest and Instagram and—"

Liberty interrupted and said, "I remember when people would simply post things to doors. For example, in 1770 I remember a posting about the Boston Massacre!"

"The mass of what?" Tommy asked.

"The Boston Massacre," Cam said.

Liberty agreed. "Yes, I saw a drawing of it that Paul Revere engraved, printed, and posted all over Boston. I suppose if Paul Revere had Facebook or Instagram he would've posted it there as well!"

"I wish I had taken a picture of King George," Elizabeth sighed as if she were daydreaming. "He looked magnificent!" Elizabeth twirled around and around as she waltzed down the hallway. "Adieu!"

I looked at Tommy and Cam, who looked as worried as I did.

"Should we try to stop her? What's going to happen when Principal Sherman sees her dress?" said Tommy.

"Yeah, she has all the evidence she needs to bust us!" Cam said.

"Let's not panic," I said. "I don't think she's in any hurry to burn the bridge that let her meet King George. I'd say she's very happy."

"I'd say she's loopy!" Cam said.

"I'd say she's nuts-o," said Tommy.

"I'd say her chimney is missing a few bricks!" said Liberty, who snorted at his own joke.

"I'd say you better get in here," said Freedom, who stuck her head out the classroom door. "The video you took of Benjamin Franklin just ended and kids are wondering where you are."

I turned to Tommy and Cam and said, "After Tommy changes his clothes I need the two of you to go to the teachers' lounge and grab the sound system and speakers. Bring them here so Liberty can perform his stomp act about the Stamp Act."

Cam started to laugh and said, "I'm sorry for laughing but it sounds really funny every time you say that."

Liberty replied, "I always laugh when I hear the question, 'How much wood could a woodchuck chuck if a woodchuck could chuck wood?' If I ever meet a woodchuck I'm going to ask him if woodchucks really do chuck wood and if so, how much wood would he really chuck if he could? I mean if he chucks too much wood could a woodchuck upchuck the chucked wood?"

The things this horse says, I thought. I smiled and pulled Liberty's halter toward the classroom door. "Let's go. It's time for Honors History," I said.

The two boys darted down the hallway and Liberty and I entered the classroom. Upon seeing us the students quickly settled down.

I walked to the front of the class and said, "We're going to have a quick test on the movie about Benjamin Franklin that you just watched. I'm going to pass out a piece of paper and I want you to answer the question, 'Why were the colonies opposed to the Stamp Act?'"

I heard a couple of moans and sighs.

I continued: "Before you answer I'll need you to give me five dollars each for the paper you're going to use to take the test."

This time I heard lots of moans, gasps, sighs, and even a "That's a rip-off!"

"Is there a problem?" I asked.

A boy in the middle of the room raised his hand and said, "It's not fair!"

And then a girl said, "Don't my parents already pay taxes for this?"

Another boy said, "Do we have to use your paper? If I use my own do I still have to pay the five dollars?"

I smiled and said, "Yes, you still have to pay the five dollars. Yes, I assume your parents are paying taxes already. And, yes, I'm requiring you to pay this paper tax because it's going to help me pay off some debts."

Now it seemed like the whole class was in an uproar.

"Mr. Revere," said Freedom from the back of the class, "this sounds a lot like the stamp tax that Parliament and the King demanded that the colonies pay. And we sound a lot like the colonists who didn't think it was fair."

"Very good, Freedom. I'm glad to know that the video you watched may have taught you something. In any case, I think Parliament and the King are right. So I need you to pay me now!"

"Seriously?" Freedom smirked, thinking I was kidding. "What if the whole class decides not to pay the tax? What if we refuse?"

"Is that how all of you feel?" I asked as I looked around the room.

"I'm with Freedom! Me, too! I'm not paying! No way! Freedom is right!" said the students until they all started chanting, "We won't pay! We won't pay! We won't pay!"

With a wide grin I finally held up my hands to quiet the student mob and said, "Congratulations, you passed the test and you all get an A!" As the class cheered, Tommy and Cam entered the room carrying the sound system and speakers. I quickly set them up and invited Liberty to come to the front of the room. With a short introduction I said, "It's my pleasure to introduce Liberty and his stomp act about the Stamp Act."

The music started, Liberty began stomping to the beat, and then he started to sing:

(Sung to the tune of "Call Me Maybe" by Carly Rae Jepsen and Tavish Crowe)
I threw a stamp on the fire
Go tell the British Empire
Your Stamp Act agents are fired
You're simply in our way

Go tell King George the III
His Stamp Act is absurd
This is our final word
You're simply in our way

This law is bogus
Taxing all our paper products
Do you really think you own us?
Listen to the Stamp Act Congress!

Hey, we just left you
And this is crazy
You never asked us
Don't tax our colonies
We've got Ben Franklin
And Patrick Henry
You never asked them
Don't tax our colonies

Because your taxes aren't fair
You make us so mad
You make us so mad
You make us so, so mad
Because your taxes aren't fair
You make us so mad
And you should know that
You make us so, so mad

As the music faded away Liberty struck a pose and the class applauded and cheered. As the bell rang, I was certain this would be a history lesson they would never forget.

The next day I had to wake up Liberty so we could have lunch before my class started. He said he was still tired and blamed it on all the time-jumping.

"Well, let's get some food in you because we'll need to time-jump today to meet Samuel Adams," I said.

Liberty yawned and replied, "Oh, I remember King George said that Samuel Adams was a rebel. Is that true?"

"Yes, Samuel Adams fanned the flames of the Revolutionary

War in Boston. He was also a cousin to the American hero John Adams. If possible I'd like to find Samuel and discover the truth. From what I've heard he was a stubborn, hotheaded, and crafty man who never doubted the cause of freedom."

"Oh, he sounds delightful," Liberty said with sarcasm.

I smiled and said, "Maybe not delightful, but he knew how to motivate people to fight for their liberties. And I want to see how he did it. I want to know what role he played in Boston and what he was truly like."

"Fine with me, but I don't think I'm adding him to my Christmas card list!"

"Well, maybe our visit will change your mind," I said.

Liberty paused before he said, "Benjamin Franklin, Patrick Henry, Samuel Adams—I'm certain I have a connection with all of these exceptional Americans but I can't seem to put my hoof on it."

"Well, you are from the revolutionary time period," I reminded him.

"Yes, I am certain of that," said Liberty. "Oh, and I'm also certain that I am famished!"

No surprise, I thought.

On our way to Manchester Middle School we stopped and ate bagels and cream cheese. Liberty ate eighteen bagels in honor of the eighteenth century.

"A full stomach always makes me sleepy," he said.

"Maybe you can take a quick nap during part of my history lesson."

As we approached the front doors of the school, Liberty turned invisible. The bell would ring at any second and students would flood the hallways as they headed toward their

A map sketched by John Adams of the taverns in Braintree and Weymouth, 1761.

□ White's

Meeting House in Weymouth

Nash's.

The public Ways in the southern Parts of
Braintree and Weymouth, are not too near
numerous perhaps if they are well provided and
well disposed, but of these Things I know nothing.

This brook divides Weymouth from Braintree

Road to South part of Braintree, & Bridgwater

□ Clark's

□ Hales

□ Braintree South Mg: House.

🏠

□ Vinton's

W

idge

Little Pond. R. Hubbards, a rather Tavern within 40 Rods of

Eng.ᵈ by W. G. Jackman

Samuel Adams

final class of the day. As we turned the final corner I saw Elizabeth slip into the Honors History classroom. I assume Liberty saw her, too, but just to be sure I said, "Did you see Elizabeth?"

Liberty exhaled and reappeared by my side. "Yes, and she looked a little sneaky. I'll stay invisible until we know what she's up to." He took a deep breath and disappeared again.

At the sound of the bell I saw students exit other classrooms along the hallway. We quickly slipped inside the Honors History room and I noticed Elizabeth sitting in her regular seat. She sweetly said, "Hello, Mr. Revere. I think we got off on the wrong foot. I've decided that Manchester Middle School definitely needs a horse, uh, I mean, a history teacher with your special skills. By the way, where's Liberty?"

She looked behind me as if she was waiting for Liberty to enter. I knew she was up to something. But what? I casually replied, "Thank you, Elizabeth. I'm glad to have you back in Honors History. Liberty will be here soon. What did Principal Sherman say about your new dress?"

"Oh, I told him I went shopping and just had to have it for the homecoming dance." She winked. "No worries, Mr. Revere. I've got you covered. I know how to play this game. You scratch my back and I'll scratch yours."

Tommy entered the classroom and paused when he saw Elizabeth.

"Hi, Thomas, did you miss me?" said Elizabeth, her words dripping with sweetness.

"No offense, but not really."

"No matter. I need to talk to you about the next time we

time-jump. The possibilities are so exciting! And I know just where I want to—"

Just then the door opened and several more students began walking in. I was relieved for the interruption. Something was definitely up with Elizabeth. She was acting very strange since our visit with King George. Finally, the bell rang for class to start and I noticed Cam was standing in the middle of the room unsure about where to sit.

"It looks like there's a desk in the middle of the classroom." I pointed to the empty desk next to Freedom. Once Cam was seated I took a quick roll call and welcomed everyone.

Liberty finally exhaled and appeared behind Freedom and Cam. I was always impressed at how long he could hold his breath and stay invisible.

I turned, grabbed a piece of chalk, and wrote on the chalkboard, "The Townshend Acts." I said, "The Stamp Act wasn't the only act or law that Parliament created and King George III approved to tax the thirteen colonies. The Quartering Act, the Declaratory Act, and numerous other acts continued to make the colonies boil with anger and hatred toward King George. But it was the Townshend Acts that may have finally pushed the colonies over the edge."

Elizabeth raised her hand and said, "You're making King George sound like a monster. Actually, he was a very nice guy with incredible taste in fashion, gorgeous blue eyes, and let's not forget, he was a king."

"Thank you, Elizabeth," I said. "But let's finish our discussion by saying that the Townshend Acts were a series of 1767 laws named for Charles Townshend, the British chancellor of

Boston. (Town of.)
Circular.

THE Merchants and Traders in this Town in the Agreement subscribed by them the 17th of *October* last, engaged that the Orders they might send for Goods to be shipped them from *Great-Britain* should be on Condition that the Acts imposing Duties for the Purpose of raising a Revenue in *America* should be totally Repealed, at the signing of which Agreement it was expected that the Merchants in *New-York*, *Philadelphia*, and other Colonies would come into a similar Agreement ; but the Merchants in the other Colonies having already ordered their Goods to be shipped in Case the Act imposing Duties on Tea, Glass, &c. is repealed, for this and other Reasons mentioned in their Letters decline concurring with us at present, but have proposed to join us in any Plan that may be thought prudent to pursue for obtaining the Repeal of the Acts of the 4th & 6th of GEORGE the Third——Therefore the Merchants here thinking it of the utmost Importance that the Traders in all the Colonies should act upon the same Plan, *have agreed to write their Correspondents that the Goods they have or may send for should be shipped on this express Condition, that the Act imposing Duties on Tea, Glass, Paper and Colours, be totally repealed, and not otherways*——And have directed their Committee to confer with the Committees of the other Colonies relative to their Proposal above-mentioned.

This Notice of the Proceedings of the Merchants, at their last Meeting, is now sent to the Gentlemen in Trade for their Government, in Case they should send any Orders for Goods.

Boston, December 6th, 1769.

Notice from Boston merchants calling for a complete
repeal of the Townshend duties, 1769.

Portrait of Charles Townshend by Joshua Reynolds.

the treasury. He's the guy keeping track of all the King's money. These laws placed new taxes on glass, lead, paints, paper, and tea. How do you think the colonies felt about paying more and more taxes?"

Cam started singing the chorus from Liberty's Stamp Act song. "Because your taxes aren't fair, you make us so mad, you make us so mad, you make us so, so mad!"

The class laughed as Cam took a bow from his seat.

"Exactly," I said. "Many of the colonists protested; sometimes they showed violence against British soldiers and the British tax collectors. So King George sent more British troops to the colonies. In fact, he sent four thousand Redcoats to the city of Boston, which only had twenty thousand residents at the time."

"It sounds like Boston was swarming with Redcoats," said Tommy.

"I wish I could take all of you back to Boston on March fifth of 1770," I said. "You'll need to use your imaginations for this. If it helps to close your eyes, please do. Daydream, if you will, to March fifth, 1770. You're in Boston, Massachusetts. It is evening and the moon is full. You're on King Street in front of the Customs Office. Street lanterns dimly light the way as you walk along the cobblestone. Eighteenth-century brick buildings and—"

Suddenly, the walls of the classroom started to spin. I leaned back onto the teacher's desk for fear that I might topple over. Was I spinning or was the room spinning? I wasn't sure. The students seemed to notice it as well. A gold and purple swirling pattern raced along the walls and encircled us until the walls completely vanished and the Bostonian scene I had just described appeared all around us. Even the cobblestone street was beneath our desks and feet. I slid my foot across the ground and it was smooth like a classroom floor, not like cobblestone.

"Mr. Revere, is this supposed to be happening?" asked Tommy.

"No worries," I said, lying. "Stay in your seats. You're experiencing, uh, a new, um, technological, uh, teaching moment . . ." I honestly had no idea what was happening. It looked like we were back in time. But that was impossible! We hadn't jumped through a portal. We would need Liberty to do that. And that's when it hit me. Liberty! This had to be his doing. I looked to the back of the room and noticed him leaned up against the back wall, fast asleep. He must be dreaming this! Somehow his subconscious had the ability to simulate the historical event I was describing! Liberty was re-creating history all around us. None of it was real but the virtual experience made us feel like we were actually there. Unbelievable! I decided to make the most of the situation and continued with my storytelling.

"Suddenly, you find yourself with a mob of people who start to throw snow, ice, and rocks at the British soldiers standing in front of the Customs Office," I said.

Sure enough, as I described the scene a large mob of colonists appeared to the right of us. To the left appeared a small group of British soldiers. A colonist stood only a few yards away from me and threw a chunk of ice. It hurtled directly at me on its way toward the soldiers. Instinctively, I winced and flinched right before the ice hit me in the side of face. But, surprisingly, the ice chunk went right through my head and continued forward, hitting the chest of a British soldier. I had forgotten this was just a simulation. It was just a virtual, holographic representation that Liberty was creating while dreaming. It seemed so real! I noticed

A broadside (poster) describing the Boston Massacre, March 5, 1770.

other students dodging snow, ice, and rocks as the projectiles flew through the air.

I continued with my narration and shouted, "The Redcoats tried to keep order and stop the colonists from demonstrating against the Townshend Acts. However, the soldiers were forbidden to shoot anyone unless they had an order from a civil magistrate who was like a judge. The Americans and Patriots knew this so they kept trash-talking and taunting the British troops. Confusion and chaos only increased when the bells began to ring from the nearby Old Brick Church."

Again, the literal sound of church bells rang through my ears as the chaos continued all around us. I knew the bell was normally used as a fire alarm in eighteenth-century Boston so it wasn't surprising when people started shouting, "Where's the fire?"

I continued: "The large, angry crowd pressed in on the nine British soldiers, who were desperately outnumbered. Suddenly, one of the British soldiers is knocked down by something hitting his head and someone yells, 'Fire!' "

The sound of gunshots ripped through the air and suddenly, the classroom walls returned as the sights and sounds of 1770 Boston vanished like a magical act.

"Oh, sorry, I must have dozed off for a minute," said Liberty, a bit startled. "Did I miss anything? The last thing I remember, you were talking about Boston and then I had the strangest dream. More like a nightmare."

"That was awesome!" said a boy in the front row.

"This class rocks!" said another boy.

"You're the best teacher ever!" said a girl sitting by the window. "How did you do that?"

Gratefully, the students seemed clueless that Liberty was the source of the simulation.

"Oh, it's, um, all high-tech cinematronics," I said, hoping it was enough.

"Seriously," said Liberty, "I feel like I missed something."

Just when I tried to get the class back on track, the school fire alarm sounded.

Principal Sherman's voice was heard on the school intercom system. He said, "Dear students, this is our annual school fire drill. Please calmly leave your classrooms and head outside to the blacktop. Thank you."

I followed the students out of the room but just before I passed through the doorway I noticed Freedom and Cam huddled with Liberty. I walked to the back of the room and asked, "I take it the three of you have something on your mind?"

"Mr. Revere," said Cam. "Since Freedom and I didn't time-travel with you last time, do you think we could go now? I'd love to go to Boston in 1770. We could learn more about the Boston Massacre!"

"I'm in!" said Freedom, enthusiastically. "We could be back before anyone realizes we're missing!"

Liberty nodded rapidly and nearly danced in place.

"All right," I said.

The three of them cheered in unison.

"You'll have to change your clothes in the past. If you run to the restroom now you may get caught by another teacher. Help me move these desks to either side of the room so we have a running path for Liberty."

In a matter of seconds we were ready to go. Freedom and Cam rode on Liberty and I followed close behind.

"Rush, rush, rushing to history!" said Liberty.

We were headed to Boston and I was excited to find Samuel Adams. I was nervous at the same time. I had just witnessed what happened in Boston on March 5, 1770. It was a dreadful day in American history, and when five Americans died and more were wounded, I knew this was the beginning of a revolutionary war.

Chapter 8

On a crisp winter morning we landed alongside a large, redbrick building. The bottom level looked like a marketplace where several merchants, fishermen, meat and produce sellers, and peddlers of every kind were selling their goods. The second level had several windows; some were opened and many voices could be heard inside.

"You realize we landed a day after the Boston Massacre, right?" Liberty said.

"Is this March sixth, 1770?" I asked.

"Yes, but you said the massacre happened on March fifth," Liberty reminded me.

"Yes, I'm aware of that," I whispered. "But I didn't want my students to witness the Boston civilians who died."

"Why is it that the past always seems colder than the future?" said Freedom. "It's freezing out here!"

I reached for my travel bag and handed Freedom and

Cam their colonial clothes. "Put these clothes over your modern-day clothes. You should be warmer with a double layer."

Freedom and Cam eagerly put on the clothes like they were racing each other.

"I want the two of you to stay close to me," I said. "Let's walk to the front of the building and see where we are."

"Why don't we just ask Liberty?" said Cam. "Isn't he supposed to have special powers that let him know when and where we are?"

Liberty closed his eyes and concentrated before saying, "We're definitely in Boston and this building is . . . I can see the name but I'm not sure I can pronounce it."

"Faneuil Hall," said Freedom. "It must be a French name."

"How did you know that?" asked Cam.

"I read Liberty's mind," Freedom said, smiling.

"You can read minds?" asked Cam with a worried expression on his face.

"Don't worry, I can only communicate with animals. But I do have X-ray vision!"

"What?!" Cam blurted out as he walked behind Liberty.

"I'm just kidding." Freedom laughed.

"But wouldn't that be cool?" Liberty said. "I wish I had X-ray vision."

"You don't need it," I said. "You have your Time-Travel Sense. Can you sense Samuel Adams in this building?"

Liberty paused and then said, "Yep, he's definitely in there."

"And Faneuil Hall is a special building," I said. "It served as the Patriot headquarters or meeting place to discuss the Stamp Act, the Boston Massacre, the tea crisis, and other British laws that burdened the colonists."

"Where's Liberty?" Freedom asked.

We turned and spotted Liberty near the front of Faneuil Hall. He was staring at what looked like a sign. We followed Liberty and as we got closer I read the sign that had caught his complete attention. It read, *Faneuil Hall Boston, the Cradle of Liberty. Dedicated in 1763 in the cause of liberty!*

"Have you ever seen anything so beautiful?" asked Liberty, who was nearly crying. "Although I don't remember sleeping in a cradle. In fact, I don't think I'd fit inside a cradle unless it was a giant one. Oh well. Hey, you should take a picture of me beside this sign!"

After a quick photo I said, "Let's look inside the building."

"What are we looking for?" asked Freedom.

"I want to meet Samuel Adams," I said. "Today, he's giving an impassioned speech about last night's horrific events."

Liberty replied, "I'm going to sit this one out. I mean I'm glad this Adams guy is on our side but I don't want to risk getting yelled at."

"Why do you say that?" Freedom asked, a little worried.

I interjected: "From what I've learned Samuel Adams is not a patient person but I'm sure he's—"

"You said he was pigheaded and needs anger-management classes," Liberty said.

"Well, I, uh, I've never actually met the man. It's just what I've read in history books," I said defensively.

"So why are we meeting him?" Cam asked.

I sighed and explained: "Samuel Adams may not have the genius and social skills of Benjamin Franklin and he may not be as brilliant and lighthearted as Patrick Henry but he definitely played an important role in America's independence. Let me tell the three of you something that I hope you never forget. You will meet people in your life that get on your nerves. Maybe they challenge your ideas or they're not willing to completely agree with you. That doesn't mean they're bad people. Yes, Samuel Adams was said to be a stubborn and quick-tempered man. But I think we'll see that he was an incredible motivator. The point is I believe that God knew He would need different people with a variety of personalities to create a free America. He needed men and women who weren't afraid to speak their minds. He needed people who would not back down. And, frankly, this country needs more of that today. Our country needs kids like you to speak up when our liberties are being threatened. Our forefathers said and did hard things even when they knew it might not be the popular thing. Samuel Adams is one of those people. He wasn't trying to win a popularity contest. He was trying to motivate people to take a stand and fight for their liberties!"

"Thanks, Mr. Revere," said Cam. "I know peer pressure makes a lot of kids go along with the crowd even when they know it's not the right thing."

"Yeah, thanks, Mr. Revere," echoed Freedom. "My mom named me Freedom because she hoped that it would give me the courage to stand up to others who might take advantage of me. I don't do a very good job at that. But now I'm anxious to meet Samuel Adams. Maybe I can pick up a few tips from him."

"No kidding," agreed Cam. "Let's go meet the Samuelator!"

"The what?" Liberty said.

"You know, like the Terminator! The Samuelator!"

"Oh, well, good luck with that. I'll meet you outside when you're finished," said Liberty.

As we entered the front doors I noticed the hall inside was

packed with people, from the entrance all the way to the plat-form on the other side. The man standing near the podium was dressed in simple colonial fashion. He looked like he was in his late forties. I immediately felt his penetrating stare, which seemed to reach all the way across the room and into my soul. When he started to speak I knew instantly that this was the exceptional American Samuel Adams. "There he is," I said.

"That's the Samuelator?" asked Cam.

"Show some respect," said Freedom. "It's Samuel Adams."

"Yes, that's him!" I said, mesmerized by what he was saying.

Samuel looked over the crowd and boldly said, "The governor of Massachusetts says that I'm the great incendiary. He says I spread lies about the British Empire and spread stories about the injustice of the King. But I will tell you that my purpose and my passion is to warn against the hostile designs of Great Britain!"

The crowded room erupted with shouts and cheers.

Samuel Adams continued: "Furthermore, I accept your nomination to chair a committee that will petition Governor Hutchinson for the immediate removal of British troops from the city of Boston!"

"Hear, hear!" shouted members of the crowd.

"America should never forget the horrid massacre in Boston," said Samuel, "when five innocent Patriots were shot by British muskets. We will honor men like Crispus Attucks, who was the first to fall, struck twice in the chest by bullets."

Again, the crowd erupted with anger. It was beginning to look and sound like a mob.

"That's harsh!" said Cam. "I remember hearing the gunshots in the classroom. I bet that's when the Patriots got shot."

"Yeah," said Freedom. "But I don't like that innocent people are getting killed."

"No kidding," said Cam, somberly. "And too bad about Crispus Attucks. I've never heard of him before."

I whispered, "History tells us that Attucks was of African and Native American descent and had fled to Boston after escaping his enslavers. In fact, he has a monument in Boston that hails him as a hero of the American Revolution, the first Patriot to give his life for the cause."

"I wonder if he would've still gone to King Street and protested like that if he knew he might die," said Freedom thoughtfully.

"That's a good question, Freedom," I said. "But I think a hero does what needs to be done and says what needs to be said despite the consequence, even if it means giving your life. That's why I consider Samuel Adams an American hero. He could have hanged for the things he said, but it didn't stop him."

As the public meeting ended we weaved our way through the crowded hall and headed toward the podium.

"We'll try to introduce ourselves to Samuel Adams. It would be great to meet him and ask a few questions," I said. "But I'm not sure I see him anymore."

"It feels like everyone's really fired up!" Freedom said.

"No kidding," Cam said. "It feels like we're at a tailgate party before a football game. It's too bad Samuel Adams can't come to a game. I bet he'd be an awesome cheerleader!"

"Oh, sure, let's invite Samuel Adams to a football game. I'm sure he doesn't have anything better to do," Freedom said, a voice of reason.

Crispus Attucks, one of the men killed in the Boston Massacre.

"And just what am I being invited to?" asked Samuel from behind us.

I could hardly believe I was standing face-to-face with the legendary Samuel Adams. I said, "Sir, Mr. Adams, Samuel or do you go by Sam, I mean, it's a pleasure to meet you. We're huge admirers of yours and fellow Patriots!"

"I'm not looking for admirers," stated Samuel. "But I am looking to grow the cause of freedom. Now, tell me about this *football* game. Is this a game for Patriots?"

"Actually, yes," laughed Cam. "The New England Patriots are a football team in Massachusetts! Personally, I like the Broncos but—"

Freedom elbowed Cam in the ribs.

I quickly tried to change the subject and said, "These are two of my students, Cam and Freedom. And I'm Rush Revere, history teacher and historian. I brought them to hear your speech and, hopefully, help them understand the importance of fighting for freedom. We were very inspired and motivated by your speech. In fact, we'd love to help support the cause any way we can."

"Your name is Freedom, you say?" asked Samuel, who turned to look at Freedom. "That is a name worth having and a cause worth fighting for."

"Well, I'm not really a fighter," said Freedom.

"Nonsense!" shouted Samuel.

His word made Freedom practically jump.

Samuel firmly said, "We were born to fight. A baby fights for his first breath! Our hearts fight to beat every second of every day. If you stood between a hungry wolf who was after a younger sister or brother and you had a club in your hand, what would you do?"

Freedom looked nervous about answering but finally said, "I would fight it off."

"What? I didn't hear you. Say it louder!" Samuel prodded.

Freedom tried again, this time a little louder: "I said, I would fight off the wolf."

"Of course you would!" Samuel said, sounding almost angry. "And King George is simply a wolf that wears a crown! Do you understand?"

"Yes," said Freedom timidly.

"Don't ever forget that you are a fighter, Freedom. You are worth fighting for."

Freedom nodded and gave a weak but sincere smile.

Samuel turned toward me and asked, "Did you say your name is Rush Revere?"

"Yes, that's right," I said and smiled.

"I am a good friend with Paul Revere, a fellow Patriot here in Boston," said Samuel. "In fact, I'm on my way to visit with him now. He is a master silversmith and I am in need of his services. Would you care to join me?"

"Really?!" I asked with wonder. "It would be a great honor to meet him as well. I'm sure we're related."

"Come, then," said Samuel, "we will travel together. His shop isn't far from here."

"Thank you! That is very generous of you," I stammered. I was practically shaking from the anticipation and excitement of meeting my favorite exceptional American, Paul Revere.

As we followed Samuel out the doors and down the stairs of

Faneuil Hall, a man who I assumed was a fellow Patriot called to speak with Samuel. Samuel stepped away briefly and as I waited I overheard bits and pieces of their conversation. Something about a secret meeting and the Sons of Liberty. Interesting.

Cam interrupted and said, "Mr. Revere, we found Liberty. He's down by those food vendors. Apparently, someone spilled a whole pot of baked beans and Liberty decided he'd help clean things up."

"Yes, cleaning up food is his specialty!" I laughed. "Tell him to hurry because we're following Samuel Adams to Paul Revere's silversmith shop.

Samuel finished his conversation about the "secret meeting" and said, "I apologize for keeping you waiting."

"Not a problem," I said. "Lead the way, Mr. Adams."

Cam and Freedom followed close behind and Freedom led Liberty by the halter. The streets of Boston were buzzing with colonists. Their mood seemed somber as they went about their errands. I noticed many dirt streets that branched off from the main cobblestone street that we traveled on. Samuel pointed out several of his favorite shops along Main Street. A tavern, a fruit vendor, a bakery, and a barbershop. A hat store, a fish market, a pipe maker, and a flower shop. Merchants lined the streets and a variety of signs hung over their doors and windows. "The Hoop Petticoat," "The Four Sugar Loaves," "The Chest of Drawers," and "The Spring Clock & Watches" were just a few of the signs that caught my eye.

"For the most part we have all the luxuries we need. England does ship goods for us to purchase but I prefer to purchase items made in America," Samuel said.

Faneuil Hall as it looked in Boston around this period.

In addition, Redcoats could be seen policing the streets. They traveled together in groups of five or six. We crossed the street whenever Redcoats were approaching. In fact, I noticed most of the colonists tried to avoid the British soldiers.

As we walked, Samuel said, "Paul Revere is a master silversmith. After he fought in the French and Indian War he took over his father's shop."

Curious, I asked, "Exactly what kinds of things does he make?"

"I don't think there's anything he couldn't make. He is a true artisan of silver."

"And is this why you are visiting Paul Revere, today? You want to purchase one of his silver pieces?" I inquired.

"No, I'm going to ask Paul to use his skills to engrave a piece of copper. You see, Paul Revere has a small printing press in his shop. Whatever he engraves on a thin piece of copper can be used as a template for his printing press. The piece of copper can be printed over and over again," said Samuel.

"And what exactly do you plan to engrave on the piece of copper?"

"You get right to the point, Rush Revere! I like that," said Samuel. "The British army has given us a golden opportunity. I have called it the Boston Massacre. In fact, we approach King Street now. This is where the tragedy occurred last night."

Overhearing our conversation, Cam said, "I recognize the Customs Office and the Old Brick Church."

Indeed, back in the classroom Liberty had dreamed a remarkable simulation of the crime scene. As we walked to the place where the crowd of colonists stood shouting at the British soldiers, I saw thin patches of snow in the shadows of the buildings. A large icicle fell from a two-story building and shattered into dozens of large chunks. A thick, jagged piece tumbled across the street until it hit my leather shoe. I looked down at the piece of broken ice and saw a large dark stain on the cobblestone. A cold wind blew across my face and gave me goose bumps. I knelt to get a better look and shivered at the thought of what had happened at this very spot last night.

Behind me, Samuel said, "I have talked to many witnesses about the event last night and it appears that the British soldiers indeed fired upon several Americans. However, I've also discovered that the Americans who gathered were not all peaceful bystanders. Most likely, some provoked and taunted the soldiers. Sticks and stones and ice were thrown at the Redcoats. The angry crowd started pressing in on the nine soldiers."

"And that's when someone shouted, 'Fire!'" I softly said, remembering the event from the classroom.

"Correct," said Samuel. "My investigation tells me that Captain Thomas Preston ordered his soldiers not to fire. However, by then it was too late. One of his men fired his musket and soon after, several more shots were fired, killing five unarmed men. It was bound to happen with the Quartering Act, quartering troops so close to the civilian population. It is like putting a fuse so close to flame."

"Perhaps both sides are guilty," I said, finally standing and looking at Samuel.

"Perhaps," said Samuel. "My cousin John Adams has been asked to defend the British soldiers who were at the massacre. Only a handful of witnesses will ever know what truly happened.

However, I'm a big believer that people will believe what we tell them, and I intend to spread the word to help spread the cause of the Patriots. We can use this to our advantage."

"And this plan involves Paul Revere," I said matter-of-factly.

"It does," Samuel said. "Paul Revere's silversmith shop is not far from here."

I looked for Cam and Freedom and saw them near Liberty. Freedom was huddled up close against Liberty's neck. I walked over and asked, "Are you cold?"

"I'm fine," said Freedom, quietly.

Cam replied, "I guess this is the ugly part of history, eh?"

"Yes," I said. "I am sorry if this was a hard thing to experience. I hadn't planned to—"

"It's okay, I'm glad we came," said Freedom. "But it's a weird feeling to think about what happened here last night."

Cam agreed. "Yeah, I know it's just a street but it feels like a cemetery."

Samuel called from across the street and said, "We must be on our way!"

A cold wind blew again across our faces. It chilled me to the bone as the image of those who lost their lives seemed to lie very near the stain-filled streets.

We continued following Samuel in silence and soon heard the sound of someone pounding metal.

"Ah, here we are. Paul Revere's silversmith shop," said Samuel.

I was glad we'd arrived. My somber mood changed to wonder as I thought about meeting the one and only Paul Revere. I straightened my coat and I felt like I was a little boy again ready to meet Santa Claus.

I peered through the shop window and noticed the most

The Boston Tea Party was planned here at the Green Dragon tavern.

beautiful, handcrafted pieces of silver I had ever seen. Spoons, cups, trays, bowls, and teapots adorned the window display.

"I like that bowl with the horse engraved on the side of it," said Freedom.

"I like it, too," whispered Liberty into Freedom's ear.

"His craftsmanship is impressive," Samuel said. "Believe it or not, he even crafted a small, silver chain for a pet squirrel."

I laughed at the thought of it.

"Seriously?" laughed Cam. "I wish I could get a picture of that!"

"Such a picture would be senseless," said Samuel, clearly not seeing the humor of it.

As Samuel opened the door I saw a man sitting behind an anvil. Hot sparks burst between the anvil and the heavy hammer each time it connected with the silver that he worked with. I could practically feel the hot furnace from the doorway and certainly smelled the melting metal. As we walked through the doorway I left the door ajar just a bit so Liberty could hear our conversation. My heart was beating fast and my palms felt cold and sweaty. I didn't realize how nervous I would feel upon meeting my boyhood hero. I had met dozens of exceptional Americans, but this one was extra special for me.

"Paul, my good friend," said Samuel, "may I introduce you to my new friends, Rush Revere and his students Cam and Freedom?"

Paul set down his hammer and wiped his brow. He looked like a strong man with broad shoulders and mighty forearms. He wore a leather apron over his linen shirt, which was rolled up at the sleeves. His hair was pulled back into a ponytail and he immediately smiled at me like we were long-lost brothers.

"With a last name like that, I'm sure you must be a brilliant man!" said Paul, laughing. "It's a pleasure to meet you." He reached out his hand and I did the same. His handshake was firm and he looked me straight in the eyes. "To what do I owe this visit?"

I said, "I am a history teacher and historian, and I have been a great admirer of all you've done for America's independence."

Paul laughed heartily and said, "I like this Revere. He speaks of our independence as if it has already happened!"

"Yes, it seems all the Reveres are true Patriots!" said Samuel. "I will tell you why I have come. But first, I must show you this drawing." Samuel unrolled a piece of parchment that he was carrying. "I asked a man by the name of Henry Pelham to draw this illustration of the massacre on King Street last night." He showed it to Paul Revere.

"Massacre?" Paul said with a surprised grin.

I found myself smiling with him and not knowing why. It's as if his smile was contagious.

Paul said, "Ha! I should not be surprised that you chose a word with such drama!" Paul laughed again. I could see that this was a man who loved life. He made me feel right at home in a way that Samuel Adams definitely didn't. He was good at his craft and his customers probably enjoyed him as much as his handiwork. Paul turned in my direction and said, "Be careful of what Samuel tells you. He is very good at spinning a story to his own benefit. Bending the truth is his specialty!" Paul slapped Samuel on the back and laughed again while Samuel grimaced. Paul continued, "The word *massacre* makes it sound like the Redcoats were premeditated and cold-blooded."

"Some of us fight with swords and some of us fight with words," said Samuel with a glint in his eye. "I call it the Boston

Massacre because I want Americans to always remember the horrific event of March fifth, 1770."

I peered at the drawing and noticed that it showed British soldiers firing at peaceful Boston citizens.

With a bit of anger Samuel said to Paul, "And why do you criticize me for lighting a fire under our fight for freedom?! My intent is to remind all Americans how unjust and unfair King George has been to the colonies. He is trying to cripple our economy by taxing everything. He wants to crush our hopes of independence. He will stop at nothing until he kills our chance for freedom."

"I agree," said Paul, smiling. "No need to bark up my tree. Boston is clearly being targeted by the British Empire. King George sends more and more troops to Boston. We must do something! I assume you have a plan? You always do," Paul said, laughing.

Samuel nodded and said, "Yes, I do. I need the help of a master silversmith to engrave this picture on a copperplate so we can print and distribute it to as many Americans as possible."

"I can do it," said Paul. "It will take some time, but I can do it."

"Well, if you cannot do it, perhaps the printer and Patriot Benjamin Franklin can?" teased Samuel with a serious look on his face.

Paul's laughter bounced off the walls of the small silversmith shop. He said, "You really know how to motivate a person!"

Surely I was biased, but I loved Paul Revere's attitude. He never seemed to doubt his own ability and he was always optimistic about getting the job done. I wished I could stay with him all day and listen to his adventures and stories.

Just then the door creaked open and Liberty stumbled inside.

Paul Revere, American Patriot (1735–1818).

Freedom whispered, "He was listening too closely and accidentally fell into the door."

"Is this your horse," Paul asked, walking to the door.

"Oh, uh, yes, I apologize. He is a curious animal, and I'm sure he was just looking for us," I said.

"I am looking for a new horse," said Paul. "Would you consider selling him?"

"No, I couldn't," I said. "We've been through a lot together."

"Before you go, I have a gift for Cam and Freedom," said Paul. He walked to the back of his shop and then returned with two silver objects. "These are whistles," said Paul, proudly. "They make a very loud, high-pitched sound. I recommend you use this in case of an emergency only." He laughed again and we all laughed with him.

I turned to Samuel Adams and Paul Revere and said, "I will forever remember this day, gentlemen. Thank you for your dedication and your bravery. As a teacher of history I will make sure your names are remembered as exceptional Americans!"

"We are far from exceptional," said Samuel seriously.

"True, but I'm a little closer than Samuel," Paul said jokingly.

As Cam and Freedom left the shop, Samuel lowered his voice and said, "I invite you to join our secret society of Patriots, called the Sons of Liberty. Paul is also a Son of Liberty. I feel I can trust you and we need good men who have the courage to fight for freedom no matter the cost."

"I'm honored," I said without hesitation. "I will find you the next time I am in town."

As we parted ways I thought about the commitment I had just made, the commitment that all the Sons of Liberty had

made. Their imprint in American history would forever be re-membered during the famous Boston Tea Party.

As I left the shop I saw Cam and Freedom sitting on Liberty's saddle. Both were plugging their noses. As I got closer to Liberty I realized why.

"What's that smell?" I asked, grimacing.

Just then Liberty tooted and said, "Excuse me. I, um, may have sampled some beans earlier and, well, let's just say I'll have plenty of gas to get us through the time portal."

I simply shook my head and smiled. It was definitely time to jump back to Manchester Middle School.

The Old State House as it looks today in Boston, Massachusetts.

Chapter 9

While we waited for the bell that signaled the end of the fire drill, Liberty quickly exited the classroom.

"Did you see the look on Liberty's face?" Cam asked as he started laughing. "So funny! He kept passing gas every time he took a step!"

"I know, right?" said Freedom with a big grin. "Even after he turned invisible we could still hear him tooting all the way down the hallway!"

Their laughter was contagious.

Tommy walked over and whispered, "I still can't believe you time-jumped without me!"

Freedom replied, "Oh, I almost forgot. This is for you." Freedom handed Tommy her silver whistle. "I'm not much of a whistle blower. And since you couldn't come, I want you to have it. Paul Revere made it."

"Wow, thanks, Freedom!" Tommy said and gave Freedom a giant grin.

When the bell rang, Freedom said, "Gotta catch my ride. Bye! And thanks again for the field trip!"

"But I'm still jealous that I didn't get to go with you guys," said Tommy to Cam.

"It just sort of happened," Cam said. "Plus, you and Elizabeth got to time-jump when you visited King George."

"Speaking of Elizabeth, I didn't see her when the class returned," I said.

"Oh, yeah," Tommy said softly. "I almost forgot. I spoke with her outside while we waited for the fire alarm to stop. She kept talking about King George III and how excited she was to see him again. I told her I didn't think we were going back there, and she said, 'Yes, we are, Thomas.' Ugh, I hate when she calls me that."

"What else did she say?" I asked.

Tommy looked around the room to make sure we were alone and said, "Ever since she came back from Windsor Castle she's been acting really strange." He did his best Elizabeth impersonation: "Oh, Thomas, it's my destiny to return to England. I have plans and they involve King George."

"Hey, you sound just like her," Cam said and laughed.

The two boys high-fived each other and Tommy said, "So, anyway, I asked her what her *plans* were. I told her maybe I could help. I was curious to know what she's up to."

"What did she say?" Cam asked.

Again, pretending to be Elizabeth, Tommy said, "Oh, Thomas, wouldn't you like to know!"

Cam raised one eyebrow and said, "On second thought, you probably shouldn't talk like that. It's sort of creepin' me out!"

Tommy chuckled. "Anyway, while we were waiting for the fire drill to end a couple of kids were throwing a football back and forth but one of their passes went wide. It soared like a heat-seeking missile headed right for Elizabeth."

"Let me guess—KABLAM!" Cam said.

"Yep, it was a direct hit! Her books and folders and papers went everywhere. As soon as those kids saw what happened they ran away like a quarterback running from a linebacker."

"I don't blame them," I said, smiling. "Elizabeth is a pretty mean linebacker!"

"Anyway, I'm not sure what came over me," said Tommy, "but I decided to help her gather her things and that's when I came across this." He pulled out a folded piece of paper that was stuffed into his pocket. "I saw the words 'Top Secret' written on it so I snatched it when she wasn't looking." He handed the paper to me.

I unfolded the note and then smoothed out the paper. The note had a few words written on three lines. The first line said, *Jump to Great Britain*. The second line said, *Impress the King*. The third line said, *Tell secret about BTP*. And underneath that were several signatures. One said, *Queen Elizabeth*. Another said, *President Elizabeth*. And a third said, *Elizabeth the Great*.

"She definitely bumped her head back in the eighteenth century. She's nuts!" Cam said.

"What does BTP stand for?" asked Tommy. "British Toilet Paper?"

Cam laughed and said, "Or maybe it stands for Boston Triple-Cream Pie? I love a good pie!"

"That's something Liberty would say," I said. "Wait a second, I think you're on to something, Cam."

"I am?" Cam replied, confused. "You think Elizabeth's secret is about a pie recipe?"

"No," I corrected. "I think her secret is about Boston. In

particular, a secret event that will happen in Boston, a big secret that involves a lot of tea!"

"Ohhhhhh," Cam said, snapping his fingers. "BTP. Boston Tea Party! Of course!"

"Exactly," I exclaimed. "If the King knew about the Boston Tea Party before it happened, well, he could probably stop it and it could be the beginning of the end of the American Revolution."

Tommy raised his hand like he was in class. "What exactly is the Boston Tea Party? And why would Elizabeth plan something like that?"

"Elizabeth isn't planning it," I said. "The Boston Tea Party is a secret mission planned by the Sons of Liberty."

"Liberty has sons?" asked Tommy, surprised.

"No, I'm referring to a secret organization called the Sons of Liberty. It was a well-organized group of Patriots who banded together to resist the British and unfair laws like the Stamp Act. The Sons of Liberty were sort of like Robin Hood and Batman mixed into one. When the colonists were burdened and suffering because of King George and his minions, the Sons of Liberty would come to the rescue! Their most famous operation was the Boston Tea Party!"

"Cool!" Tommy was smiling. "I wish I could be a Son of Liberty. What else did they do, Mr. Revere?"

"They once tried to persuade Governor Thomas Hutchinson of Massachusetts to reject the Stamp Act in his official letters to London. The governor was a loyalist so, of course, he refused. In fact, Governor Hutchinson sent and received many letters to and from England. These letters made it very clear that the British were superior. King George and his Parliament thought the colonists were sloppy and stupid so they granted fewer rights to people living in America. Simply, the letters said that Britain was better and America was blech! Governor Hutchinson agreed and that made the Sons of Liberty really mad so they attacked the governor's mansion. They axed his door, uprooted his garden, and destroyed much of his home. Of course, they didn't harm the governor, but they told him that he didn't belong in America. Eventually, he left Massachusetts and returned to England."

"Okay, wait, back up," said Tommy. "You said the Sons of Liberty were the ones who planned the Boston Tea Party. A tea party? I don't get it. I mean, my little sister likes to have tea parties with all her friends. I just don't see the Sons of Liberty doing that."

Cam laughed. "Not that kind of tea party!" he said.

I laughed as well and said, "The best way for me to explain it is to simply show you!"

"Awesome!" Tommy said. "Road trip!"

"Let's go find Liberty," I said.

"Yeah, it shouldn't be too hard to find him." Cam smiled. "All we have to do is to listen for someone cutting the cheese!"

Tommy chuckled and asked, "Seriously?"

"Oh yeah," said Cam. "He ate a boatload of beans in Boston."

After fifteen minutes, we found Liberty. He was waiting for us by the big oak tree near the back door of the school.

"Is everything okay?" I asked.

"Let's just say I've *bean* better," Liberty said with a half smile.

"Are you up to jumping again?" I asked Liberty.

"Did the *Mayflower* make it to the New World? Did Benjamin Franklin invent the lightning rod? Was Paul Revere a master blacksmith?" asked Liberty.

"I think he means *yes*," said Cam.

All the students and buses had left by now, and the schoolyard

A broadside (poster) calling the Sons of Liberty to a meeting at twelve o'clock on December 17, 1765.

looked deserted. After Tommy and Cam climbed up onto Liberty's saddle, Liberty said, *"Rush, rush, rushing to history!"*

Swirling colors of purple and gold grew to the size of a Hobbit hole. As we rushed to the time portal I said, "December sixteenth, 1773, Boston, Massachusetts, the Old South Meeting House!" We jumped and the next thing I felt was the chilled air. Were we in a field or a park? It was hard to tell since the only light came from the moon and the flickering lanterns and candles in a building straight ahead of us. It looked like an old church with a large steeple that stood like a single sentinel keeping watch over the large crowd of colonists below. The boys quickly jumped off Liberty and put on their colonial clothes over their modern-day clothes.

"There must be five thousand people over there," said Tommy.

I nodded. "We're about to witness another key event that brings the thirteen colonies that much closer to their revolution against Great Britain."

"Can we get a closer look?" asked Cam. "I want to hear what they say."

As we approached the front doors to the meetinghouse a man rushed outside and pushed his way through the crowd. He wore cream-colored breeches and white stockings as well as a cream-colored vest buttoned nearly to the neck. His royal blue coat with golden buttons and gold trim hung low to his knees and reminded me of something a ship's captain would wear. The man was searching for something. When he saw us he hurried over and said, "I'm in need of a swift horse. I'm Mr. Francis Rotch, owner of the *Dartmouth* out of England. I've been asked to seek a pass from Governor Hutchinson so my ship might return to England with its crates of tea. May I borrow your horse? I expect to return shortly with the governor's answer."

Before I could respond, Liberty was enthusiastically nodding his head. He looked excited for this unexpected adventure. I knew Liberty was a fast horse and would enjoy the task of an important mission. I finally said, "Oh, why not?"

"Thank you, my good sir. I shall return shortly," said Francis. Within seconds he was sitting in Liberty's saddle and dashing off into the night.

I turned to the boys and said, "Let's squeeze our way into the meetinghouse."

"I think the *Dartmouth* is the name of a ship," said Cam.

"Yes, that's right," I confirmed. "The *Dartmouth* is one of three ships that are sitting in Boston Harbor right now with hundreds of crates of tea from England. King George and Parliament are trying to force the colonists to purchase only British tea. In fact, the King has made his tea cheaper than anything else the colonists could buy."

"Yeah, but he's also making the colonists pay a tax on the tea!" said Cam.

"More taxes?" asked Tommy. "King George doesn't give up! I mean, it's pretty obvious the colonies don't want to be taxed by England anymore. You'd think the King would've learned that lesson with the Stamp Act!"

"History shows that King George III was not a very smart man," I said.

"Okay, but wait a second," said Tommy. "The guy who rode off on Liberty said that his ship can't leave the harbor without a pass from the governor?"

"That's right," I said. "You see, the *Dartmouth* arrived in Boston a few weeks ago. A tax has to be paid the moment the cargo of tea is removed from the ship. However, the colonists refuse to pay the tax and, therefore, don't want the tea to leave the ship.

THE

Boston- AND **Gazette,**

COUNTRY **JOURNAL.**

Containing the freshest Advices, *Foreign and Domestic.*

No. 769.

MONDAY, *January* 1, 1770.

A LIST of the Names of *those* who AUDACIOUSLY continue to counteract the UNITED SENTIMENTS of the BODY of Merchants thro'out NORTH-AMERICA; by importing British Goods contrary to the Agreement.

John Bernard,
(In King-Street, almost opposite Vernon's Head.

James McMasters,
(On Treat's Wharf.

Patrick McMasters,
(Opposite the Sign of the Lamb.

John Mein,
(Opposite the White-Horse, and in King-Street.

Anne & Elizabeth Cummings,
(Opposite the Old Brick Meeting House, all of Boston.

And, **Henry Barnes,**
(Trader in the Town of Marlboro'.

HAVE, and do still continue to import Goods from London, contrary to the Agreement of the Merchants.—They have been requested to Store their Goods upon the same Terms as the rest of the Importers have done, but absolutely refuse, by conducting in this Manner.

IT must evidently appear that they have preferred their own little private Advantage to the Welfare of America: It is therefore highly proper that the Public should know who they are, that have at this critical Time, sordidly detached themselves from the public Interest; and as they will be deemed Enemies to their Country, by all who are well-wishers to it; so those who afford them their Countenance or give them their Custom, must expect to be considered in the same disagreeable Light.

On WEDNESDAY Next the 3d Inst.

At TEN o'Clock in the Morning, Will be Sold by PUBLIC VENDUE, at the Store of the late Mr. JOHN SPOONER, next Door Eastward of the Heart and Crown.

All his Warehouse Goods,

Consisting of a large Quantity of KNIVES and Forks, Cutteos, Shoe Knives, Butchers Knives, all kinds of Pen-knives, all kinds of Shears and Scissars, Borax, Fountain Pens, Pins, Needles, Razors, Temple and Bow Spectacles, Hand Saws, all sorts Carpenters Irons and Chizzels, Brass Ladles, Skimmers, Brass Candlesticks, Steel Spring Tobacco Boxes, Handles and Escutcheons, Flatirons, Frying Pans, Rubstones, Pewter Tankards, Quart and Pint Pots, Porringers and Tea Pots; all kind of Locks, HL and other Hinges, Compasses, Squares and Rules, Bell-metal and Brass Skillets, Brass Kettles made and un-made, Shoe and Carpenters Hammers, Fire Arms, Pistols, Stone Sleeve Buttons set in Silver, large and small Fish Hooks, Gimblets, Tobacco-Tongs, Pincers, Awl & Awl Blades, Brass head & other Andirons, Steel and Brass Thimbles, Knitting Needles, Horn and Ivory Combs, Mathewman's Buttons, Beams, Scales and Weights, &c. &c. *A four Wheel Carriage.*

The Sale to continue from Day to Day 'till the whole is Sold.   J. RUSSELL, Auctioneer.

BOSTON, 23th of December, 1769.

RUN-away from the Snow Union, John Copithorn, Master, from Bristol, James Clifford and Nicholas Gries, two Seamen.—This is to desire they will return to their Duty, and they shall be well received.—If they do not, to forewarn all Persons from entertaining them, as they may expect being prosecuted according to Law.

CHARLESTOWN, (*South-Carolina,*) *Nov.* 27.

Mr. Gondacre of the 9th regiment, was not killed in a duel with a gentleman from Pensacola, as formerly mentioned, but wish Mr. G—— of the same regiment, who remains there to take his trial. The deceased declared himself the aggressor, and that his antagonist was not in the least blameable.

Nov. 9. At a meeting of the general committee on Tuesday last, and an adjournment thereof to Yesterday several matters of importance respecting the general agreement entered into by the inhabitants of this province on the 2d day of July last, were taken into consideration; and a committee of inspection appointed, whose particular business it will be, to see such Goods stored or re-shipped, (at the Option of the importer) as may be brought here contrary to the true intent and meaning of the said agreement. It was at the same time agreed, that the general committee do meet on Tuesday in every week.

We have the pleasure to inform our readers, that Mr. Thomas Eveleigh, who arrived here last Sunday, has readily agreed, that the goods which he imported in the Flora, Captain Carter, from Bristol, shall be re-shipped or stored; and that Mr. Andrew Marr, has done the same, in regard to a consignment of goods by the Brigantine Matty, arrived from Glasgow.

The subscribers to the resolution are so conscious of the justness of their proceedings, that they appear determined to adhere to them; and have not only refused to purchase some slaves lately arrived from Pensacola, but also rejected a parcel of rice, belonging to a gentleman on John's island, who is a non-subscriber.

The few interested individuals in the colonies of Rhode-island and Georgia, who have hitherto misled those unhappy colonies by skim'd milk reasonings, which has been attempted even in our province, we hear, have begun to lose so much of their influence

On Monday, January 1, 1770, the *Boston Gazette* published a list of merchants who imported British goods into Boston despite the boycott.

And to make matters worse, two more ships have arrived with more tea! So the Patriots, the colonists who are fighting for a free America, have posted guards around all the ships so that not a single crate is removed. They want the ships to return to England. But only the governor can approve such a thing."

"I get it. They want the governor to tell the King to go jump in a lake because they're not paying the stinkin' royal tea tax!" said Cam.

"In manner of speaking, yes. But the governor is not a Patriot. He's a loyalist, remember? He's supports the King. So, I'm afraid Liberty will return with bad news for the Patriots."

As we entered the front door Cam said, "There's a great spot for us to the right in the corner." There was standing room only so we shuffled across the wooden floor and squeezed our way over and against the back wall near the corner of the room. I immediately recognized Samuel Adams at the front of the large gathering. Just seeing him reminded me of his clever plan to use the Boston Massacre as a way to incite the colonists to hate Great Britain. He was always ready to get the Patriots fired up to fight against the British Empire. Tonight was no different. He was standing behind a podium with a firm scowl. He raked his fingers through his wild hair and then tried to get the attention of the raucous crowd, but the men in the room were arguing and yelling with each other. The sound was deafening and the smell reminded me that underarm deodorant hadn't been invented yet. It might have been chilly outside but it was warm and stuffy inside.

"Gentlemen, order! We will have order!" Samuel demanded. Finally, the crowd calmed down, and Samuel pointed to a man who was sitting in the balcony.

"Three pence a pound is a small sum to pay for tea!" said the man, who was surely a loyalist.

222222

"It's not the cost that angers me. It is the tax that comes with the tea!" yelled a Patriot. "I will not pay it. The tea tax is an insult to the citizens of Boston! The British Empire does not treat us as equals! We have no representation in Parliament! They think we are fools, children, and worse—slaves!"

Cam rolled his eyes and said, "Ironic, isn't it?"

"Indeed," I said.

"But we must pay for the French and Indian War debt!" yelled a loyalist. "If not for the King we might all be speaking French!"

Tommy whispered, "What does he mean by that?"

I whispered back, "King George sent thousands of British troops to help the colonists fight the French and Indians. Without the King's help the colonies would not have been able to defend their lands and defeat the French. The King wants the colonies to help pay for the war. That's partly why he's taxing them. The colonies believe they did pay for the war; many gave their lives for it. But the King and Parliament feel like the colonies still owe England."

"And that's why the King is taxing them," said Tommy.

"Correct," I said. "But as you can see and hear, the colonists can't agree on what's best for America."

"Sort of like the Senate and the House of Representatives in Congress today," said Cam with a smirk. "When our leaders can't agree, well, it can lead to a government shutdown!"

I nodded sadly. "Yes, you're getting a taste of our future government in this very room."

Although it was cold outside, the meetinghouse was getting very warm, the crowd was getting louder, and some men started shoving and pushing to get their point across.

"Mr. Revere!" Tommy shouted. "Maybe we should leave."

The idea was a good one, I thought. Unfortunately, we were

boxed into a corner with Patriots and loyalists on either side of us who looked like they were ready to come to blows.

Samuel Adams tried to retain order but he looked just as angry as the rest of them. It was apparent that neither side was willing to back down.

"We should have the right to tax ourselves and keep it in the colonies! Not send it to the King!" said a Patriot.

"And we must not let the tea leave the ships!" said another Patriot. "Our colonies in Charleston, New York, and Philadelphia all refused to accept the tea shipments. Boston must do the same!"

Suddenly, the owner of the *Dartmouth* rushed back into the assembly and yelled, "I have news from the governor!" He panted and said, "He is not willing to send the tea back to England. He said it must be landed and the tea tax must be paid!"

Patriots shouted with anger and loyalists yelled in support of what the governor had decided. It was so loud I could barely hear my own voice. I yelled to Tommy and Cam again, "Stay close by me. This could get ugly!"

"This is like a Boston Bruins ice hockey brawl!" said Tommy.

Samuel Adams raised his hands to quiet the crowd but without success. He looked like he was ready to explode.

"Hey, I have an idea!" said Cam. He pulled out the silver whistle that Paul Revere gave him.

"Good idea," said Tommy, who pulled out the whistle that Freedom gave him.

"On the count of three," Cam said.

They each put the tip of their whistle in their mouths. Cam counted to three with his fingers. One, two, three! After a deep breath the boys blew as long and as loud as they could. A high-pitched sound sliced through the room like a hot knife through

butter. The sirenlike sound seemed to bounce off the Old South Meeting House walls until all eyes turned toward Cam.

Cam smiled and said, "I think Mr. Samuel Adams has something to say."

With gratitude, Samuel nodded at Cam but he was in no mood to smile. With a stern expression on his face he looked out across the crowd of Patriots and loyalists and said, "It is clear that we are divided among ourselves. I will say only this, gentlemen. This meeting can do nothing more to save the country!" With that, Samuel Adams left the platform of the meetinghouse and slipped out the back door.

I felt someone tap me on the shoulder. As I turned I saw that it was my hero Paul Revere. "Come," he said. "Samuel said the secret words '*This meeting can do nothing more to save the country!*' We agreed that if and when he said these words the Sons of Liberty would meet behind the Old South Meeting House."

Tommy smiled and said, "Is it time for the Boston Tea Party?"

Paul looked at Tommy and while raising his eyebrows said, "Yes, that is correct." He turned his gaze toward me and said, "Rush Revere, you agreed to be a Son of Liberty, did you not?"

"Uh, yes, I did," I said.

Paul smiled and slapped me on the back. "Good, the Sons of Liberty need good men like you. And your students are welcome to join us."

"Awesome!" said Tommy. He turned to Cam and said, "You can be Robin Hood and I'll be Batman."

"No way," argued Cam. "You're Robin Hood and I'm Batman."

Paul Revere interrupted, "Robin Hood is a legendary hero who fights to destroy tyranny. A bat is a creature that cowers in caves and spreads filth and disease."

In unison, Tommy and Cam said, "I'm Robin Hood!"

"I approve. The Sons of Liberty are very much like Robin Hood of Sherwood Forest. Come, follow me," Paul said.

We scurried along the wall and then through and around several men who were still arguing about what should be done with the tea. In less than a minute we had reached the back door. We exited and found ourselves in the middle of forty or fifty Indians. No, they weren't real Native Americans, but their faces were covered with red and black war paint. They had feathers in their hair and many carried hatchets. Some were still in the process of changing from colonist to Indian, including Samuel Adams.

"We need to change our appearance," said Paul, smiling. "Come, we have enough clothes for the three of you."

I was thrilled to join the Sons of Liberty, disguised as Mohawk Indians in a unified act against the British Empire.

Cam turned to Tommy and whispered, "Dude, do you realize what we're about to do? We're going undercover! We're like eighteenth-century special ops or Navy SEALs!"

"Except we don't have night vision goggles," said Tommy. "But this is way better than playing a video game! I mean we're actually here in 1773 Boston! And we're about to be a part of history!"

"Yeah," said Cam. "Operation BTP, here we come!"

"This is going to be so awesome!" squealed Tommy.

In a few minutes we were all dressed like Indians. Well, sort of. It was a good thing it was dark, because in the daylight I bet we looked more like Peter Pan's lost boys. In any case, we used coal dust to darken our faces and arms.

"I'm just glad it's not too cold tonight or I'd be freezing," Cam said.

"I think I'll grab a couple of feathers for Liberty," I said. "I'm sure he's close and I bet he'll want to join us if he can."

Samuel Adams joined us as others formed a circle around him. Firmly, he said, "Tonight we send a message to the King. If his ships will not leave Boston so be it. But we will toss his tea overboard and let it float back to England!" Then Samuel let out a loud war whoop.

Many other war whoops echoed in response as we began marching down to Griffin's Wharf, where the three ships, the *Dartmouth*, the *Eleanor*, and the *Beaver*, were moored. Men shouted and cheered us on as we hurried down Milk Street. "Boston Harbor will be a tea pot tonight!" yelled a Patriot who slapped me on the shoulder as I passed by.

The moon overhead was bright and I was amazed at how well I could see. Was this a bit of divine intervention? Perhaps God provided the perfect weather and the perfect moon for what I hoped was a perfect tea party. Soon we were at the wharf and I felt a cold breeze come off the water and into my face. It was dark and hard to see who might be looking at us. I could barely see the faces of the other Sons of Liberty dressed as Mohawk Indians. It was a little spooky, especially hearing the creaking and squeaking of the boats as the sea pushed their hulls back and forth against the docks. It was like the three ships were trying to warn the British army. *Danger!* squeaked the *Dartmouth*. *Look! Thieves!* creaked the *Beaver*. *Don't let them take our precious chests of tea!* groaned the *Eleanor*.

Within minutes we were divided up into three different groups and ready to board the three different ships.

Suddenly, Liberty appeared out of nowhere and said, "Let's get the party started!"

"Liberty!" we all shouted, excited that he had joined us.

"It just wouldn't be the same without you," Tommy said.

"Here, let me attach these feathers to your mane. Now you're an Indian horse," I said.

I would've joined you earlier but I was speaking with Freedom. You know, with my mind."

"Wow, that's amazing," said Tommy. "I didn't think that would be possible once we passed through the time portal."

"Neither did I," said Liberty. "But our connection has been getting stronger and stronger."

"And what did Freedom have to say?" I asked.

"Oh, she just asked how I was feeling after eating all those beans. She was genuinely concerned about my well-being. That's what I like most about Freedom. Well, that and also her name. Hey, maybe that's why we have such a strong connection! Freedom and Liberty sort of go together, if you know what I mean!"

"Here come Samuel Adams and Paul Revere," I interrupted. "It looks like they'll be joining us on the *Dartmouth*."

Liberty sighed, "I'm just relieved we're not boarding the *Eleanor*. Seriously, I once had a great-aunt Eleanor who loved to suck on garlic."

"Did you say *suck* on garlic?" Tommy asked.

"Oh yeah," Liberty said. "She said it kept away the vampires!"

"Vampires?" Tommy said, doubtfully.

"Well, vampire bats. Yeah, she was a strange old mare who would stay up all night watching for bats. I guess you could call her a night-mare!" Liberty started laughing and stomping his hoof. "Get it? Nightmare! Oh, I am so funny!" he whispered as Samuel Adams and Paul Revere drew near.

"It is midnight," said Samuel. He looked up at the starlit sky and said, "It appears that heaven smiles down upon us. Yet there is still great danger. The British are all around us. Have a prayer in your heart that we shall be undetected. We must work quickly and finish before dawn."

Tommy raised his hand and asked, "What if one of those warships sees us? What if a troop of Redcoats catches us throwing the King's tea overboard?"

"I know," said Cam. "I still remember what happened to me back in Virginia. They'll cuff us until they can hang us!"

Samuel stared at Tommy and Cam for a moment as all the men around us were listening. He finally said, "I believe God wants men to be free. I choose to believe that there is a force greater than our own here tonight. I can feel it in the air and see it in the stars. God willing, we will accomplish this mission. It is only the beginning of what we will need to do. Fear will try to stop us, but we will not let it. People who live with fear will never be free. Remember this, Tommy and Cam: We are the fear chasers. We are the hope givers. We are the freedom builders. We are the Sons of Liberty!"

I felt invigorated by Samuel's words! I felt unstoppable, like I could accomplish anything. I could see that the men with me felt the same way. Even Tommy and Cam looked ready to take on the world.

Cam fumed and punched his fist into his palm. "Seriously, after what those Redcoats did to me back in Virginia with Patrick Henry, I can't wait to get my hands on that tea!"

"It's tea time!" whispered Liberty.

We walked across the gangplank of the ship and joined the other "Indians." Some were breaking open chests with hatchets to get to the tea. Since we didn't have any hatchets, Liberty kicked open a chest with his back legs and the three of us jettisoned the tea into the water below. It was too dark to see much but up close I saw thousands of little green tea leaves flitting down to the water and creating a sea of tea in the harbor below. Tea party, indeed! A really big one! Maybe some of the fish thought the tea leaves were fish flakes and decided to make a meal of it.

As Liberty stomped and kicked he softly sang his Stamp Act song, "Because your taxes aren't fair, you make us so mad, and you should know that, you make us so, so mad!"

I kept looking over my shoulder at the docks to see if any Redcoats had spotted us. The noise we were making as we busted up the wooden crates seemed loud, but it was hard to know how far-reaching it was.

After nearly four hours, we had finished. I remembered from history that there were 342 chests or crates of tea. King George would be furious when word got back to him. And you know what? I was okay with that. After all, he did insult my mother.

"I think that's the last of it," said Cam.

"Now I know what you mean by the Boston Tea Party!" said Tommy.

Cam nodded and said, "Did you see Paul Revere? That dude is strong! It must be from being a blacksmith because he was smashing through those chests like they were made of graham crackers!"

"Does someone have graham crackers?" Liberty asked. "I love graham crackers!"

"Shh," I said, patting Liberty's neck. "Here comes Paul Revere."

"Well done!" Paul said with a huge grin on his face. "The *Beaver* has also finished dumping its tea and I expect to hear word about the *Eleanor* soon."

In the light of the moon we silently rejoiced in our success, and I silently thanked God.

"So what's next?" asked Tommy.

"The King will not let this act go unpunished," said Paul. "Certainly, he will try to make an example out of Boston's rebellion. We need to do what we can to store food and supplies for our families. I would not be surprised if the King chose to close our ports. We must ready ourselves for England's retribution."

I was still in awe by the fact that I was standing just inches away from the legendary Paul Revere. I mustered up my courage and said, "Thank you, Paul Revere, for what you've done and what you'll do for this country. I don't know how you find the time to do all that you do to support the cause of freedom."

Paul beamed at my compliment. He said, "Rush Revere, you are a good man and I am honored we share the same name. Freedom is in your blood. It is in the blood of every true American. It is part of who we are. And freedom needs our effort. It needs our attention. It we are not watchful, freedom can and will be taken from us." Paul breathed deeply and exhaled. He looked deep in thought and said, "Only when we are free can we be all that God wants us to be. Only when we are free can we do all that God wants us to do. Remember this, my friend, freedom is from God. And when we fight for freedom we always fight on the side of God."

"Thank you, Paul," I said, humbly. "I will always remember that. Godspeed."

We parted ways and after leaving our boat we found an empty street and time-jumped back to Manchester Middle School. The boys changed their clothes, cleaned their faces, and walked home together. I, too, changed from my Indian attire and was glad to be back in my colonial clothing. However, Liberty left the feathers in his hair. He said he was excited to show Freedom.

I thought about tomorrow and remembered that it would be

my last day before Mrs. Borrington returned. I knew there was still one more important history lesson I wanted to teach before leaving. The fact is, England was not going to give up. And the thirteen colonies would not be able to withstand the power and might of Great Britain unless they united together. Let's face it, Boston, Massachusetts, was getting beat up pretty badly. Other colonies would experience the same punishment from the bully of Britain, King George III. I wanted Tommy, Cam, Freedom, and, yes, even Elizabeth to understand that America's freedoms were hanging by a thread. And King George was ready to take his sword and cut us off from freedom forever. Our only chance, our only hope was to unite with the other colonies and fight back. I wanted them to see and experience what really happened! For that to happen I would need to get them to the First Continental Congress.

We were just about to leave the classroom when a note was slid under the door. I walked over and picked it up. The writing on the front said, "To: Mr. Revere. From: Elizabeth." I'd forgotten about Elizabeth's secret plan to leak information about the Boston Tea Party. All she needed was someone who could open the time portal. If she could go back in time she could rewrite the history we had just experienced. And a personal visit with King George before the BTP happened could certainly do that. Well, I wouldn't let that happen. I knew I had the upper hand because I knew what she was plotting. Then again, Elizabeth was both clever and crafty. Maybe this was all a setup. Maybe she had something else up her sleeve.

Chapter 10

The next morning I did just what Elizabeth's note asked me to do. Liberty and I arrived at Manchester Middle School thirty minutes before school started. In addition, I texted Tommy, and only Tommy, to meet us near the big oak tree at the back of the school.

The back door of the school opened and Elizabeth walked out. She was dressed in the blue gown that she'd received from King George III. Her hair was expertly curled and pinned to the top of her head. She looked like a fairy princess; all she was missing was a magical wand.

"Where's Thomas?" said Elizabeth, sounding annoyed.

"Good morning, Elizabeth," I said. "You look especially pretty today. Is there a special occasion?" Of course, I knew she intended to time-jump to eighteenth-century England and visit with King George III.

"As a matter of fact, yes, there is a special occasion," she said. "And you're my ride."

"Sorry I'm late," said Tommy, who sounded a little winded. "I practically ran the whole way here."

Elizabeth sighed, "Ugh, I hope you're not sweaty."

Tommy lifted one of his arms and smelled under his armpit. "Nope," he said, "I still smell like an ocean breeze. At least that's what my deodorant said."

Liberty turned to smell Tommy's armpit as well.

"That's disgusting!" Elizabeth said.

Liberty replied, "I think you smell way better than an ocean breeze. Seriously, sometimes the breeze from the ocean smells like dead fish. I'm just saying that I don't think the person who picked the name of that deodorant has ever been to the ocean."

Elizabeth sighed and said, "Thomas, help me get in the saddle. And make sure my dress doesn't get snagged!"

"Pardon me, Elizabeth," I said, "but I don't remember us discussing any sort of field trip."

"Mr. Revere," said Elizabeth, sounding bothered by my question, "I thought we'd been over this once. I'm in charge, remember? I have the video of all of you time-jumping, so if you want to keep teaching the Honors History class you'll do what I say, and don't ask questions."

"Somebody woke up on the wrong side of the barn," Liberty mumbled.

I pondered the situation and an idea popped into my head. I called for Tommy. "You better get dressed in your colonial clothes," I told him.

As Tommy walked over to get his clothes I whispered in his ear, "When I give you the signal tell Liberty to ignore whatever Elizabeth says and concentrate on time-jumping to Philadelphia, October 1774, Carpenters' Hall."

"What's taking you guys so long?" Elizabeth huffed.

"Got it," Tommy whispered back as he finished buttoning up his vest.

Tommy quickly climbed up onto Liberty's saddle and we both helped Elizabeth to sit behind him.

"Let's go, Liberty! Open the time portal," Elizabeth said impatiently.

"Aren't you going to tell us where we're going?" Liberty questioned.

"I'll give you the destination when you're ready to jump," Elizabeth said slyly.

She was a sneaky girl. But I was not going to allow her to time-jump to England and divulge future secrets to King George. I knew her plan was to change history and I couldn't let that happen. I said, "This meeting can do nothing more to save the country!" I hoped Tommy remembered that this was the secret signal.

"Huh?" Liberty said, confused.

"Hey, that's what Samuel Adams said as . . . oh, I get it!" Tommy said. He leaned over and whispered into Liberty's ear.

"My destiny awaits!" said Elizabeth. "Giddy-up. Charge! Let's go already."

Liberty started to gallop and said, "*Rush, rush, rushing to history!*"

As we approached the time portal Elizabeth yelled, "England, November 1773, Windsor Castle."

The next second we jumped through a cosmic curtain of purple and gold and landed near a two-story colonial brick building. Other colonial buildings could be seen nearby and it was obvious that we were not at Windsor Castle, or in England for that matter. The primitive plaza was nothing like the grandiose gardens of England. And the few people we saw wore simple coats or dresses, not the fancy fashions of eighteenth-century England. The cold breeze whipped through the plaza and up through the nearby trees. Mother Nature had been busy painting the leaves a bright orange, a brilliant yellow, and a vibrant red. The leaves clung to nearby branches as they spastically fluttered in the wind.

"Where's the castle? This isn't England. You imbecile! Ugh! Where are we and what year is this?!" Elizabeth demanded.

"As your time-travel tour guide I'm obligated to tell you that we're in Philadelphia, Pennsylvania, and it's October twenty-sixth, 1774," said Liberty.

"What!" Elizabeth yelled. "Are you deaf? I specifically said Windsor Castle. It's supposed to be November 1773!" She took a deep breath and tried to calm herself. With a venomous tone she said, "I'm going to give you one more chance to get this right. Liberty! Open the time portal!"

"I'm afraid he won't do that," I said. "You see, Elizabeth, we know your plan to meet with King George and leak information about the Boston Tea Party."

Elizabeth scowled and said, "Get me off this thing!"

I quickly helped Elizabeth down from the saddle. She folded her arms and said, "You found my note, didn't you?" She looked back and forth between Tommy and me. Finally, she said, "I confess. You caught me. But it doesn't change anything."

"Yes, it does," blurted Tommy.

"Oh, my dear Thomas," said Elizabeth like she was speaking to five-year-old. "You can't stop a falling star from streaking across the sky. You can't stop an avalanche once it's racing down

NEW
HAMPSHIRE
MASSACHUSETTS
NEW YORK
RHODE ISLAND
CONNECTICUT
PENNSYLVANIA
NEW JERSEY
ATLANTIC OCEAN
DELAWARE
VIRGINIA
MARYLAND
NORTH
CAROLINA
SOUTH
CAROLINA
GEORGIA

N
W   *E*
S

The 13 Original Colonies

a mountain. And you can't stop me from reaching the greatness I was born to reach. I really should be thanking you because with Liberty I can reach that greatness a lot faster."

"You were really going to tell the King about the Boston Tea Party?" Tommy asked.

"Duh!" said Elizabeth. "It wasn't going to hurt anyone. And I would look like a hero to King George! I bet he would've given me a crown or at least a title and I could have a hundred dresses just like this one!" She twirled around and watched her dress fluff out as she spun.

"It's all about you, isn't it?" said Tommy.

"Double-duh!" said Elizabeth. "But it could be about us! Help me reach King George and I'll tell him to reward you, too!"

"I'm sorry, Elizabeth, but I would never sacrifice the future of America for my own gain or needs," I said.

"I'm with Mr. Revere," said Tommy, firmly.

"Ugh, you're such losers!" Elizabeth whined.

"Well, you were trying to ruin the Boston Tea Party and stop it from happening so technically you're captain of the losers," said Liberty as he stuck his tongue out at her.

"That's enough, you two," I said. "We've arrived at a very important time in America. History tells us that the King and Parliament were furious about the Boston Tea Party. In fact, the King was so mad he punished the colonists by closing Boston Harbor so ships weren't allowed to leave or enter."

"How did families get food?" Tommy asked, concerned.

"Sister colonies were able to send some food and supplies," I said. "But many families suffered with many men out of work. And the Redcoats swarmed Boston like red army ants."

"Good! I hope the King locks up the whole city!" said

Elizabeth. "He should ground everyone, feed them cooked spinach, and put coal in their Christmas stockings!"

"That's a bit cruel," Liberty said, "especially the cooked spinach part! Seriously, why do people ruin perfectly good spinach by cooking it?"

"Liberty," I interrupted, "we're in the middle of an important conversation."

"Oh, sorry. I'll let you and the Grinch finish," Liberty said.

"As I was saying—" I turned to Elizabeth. "The Grinch, err, I mean, the King definitely punished the Bostonians. When the other colonies heard what the King was doing they were really mad."

"No kidding!" said Tommy. "I mean King George really is the Grinch and he ticks me off big-time! I'm surprised the colonists didn't freak out earlier. Seriously, I'm not a colonist but I don't have to be to know why they're so angry! The King doesn't let them vote! He taxes everything! He sends troops into their homes and harasses them on the streets! His laws are stealing the people's hard-earned money and causing families to go hungry! And he doesn't care who he's hurting! He's not a king. He's a tyrant, thief, whiner, jerk, and a bully. Sorry, Elizabeth, but King George is the biggest loser! He's out of control and he's got to be stopped!"

Elizabeth just looked away, nearly expressionless, with her arms folded.

"Tommy," I said, "I'm very glad you understand the real issue here. In fact, the colonies have banded together in Philadelphia to fight back. Representatives, called delegates, from each of the colonies except for Georgia have come together here to decide what the colonies should do."

"Sweet!" said Tommy with wide eyes. "Is that why we're here? Is it a secret meeting? Do I know anybody that's coming? Is there a secret handshake? I wish Cam was here!"

I chuckled at Tommy's wild enthusiasm. I nodded. "Tommy, you are about to meet some of the most educated, intelligent, skillful, and courageous men in America. In fact, they are gathered in that redbrick building in front of us." I pointed to Carpenters' Hall. "They are attending the First Continental Congress."

"Awesome!" said Tommy.

"Exciting!" said Liberty.

"Boring!" complained Elizabeth. "I'm tired of you babbling on about the colonists fighting back. I insist that we visit King George this instant! Or else!"

"What are you going to do?" Tommy asked, smiling. "You don't have much leverage without your blackmail video."

Elizabeth huffed and puffed with exasperation. She finally said, "Just wait until we get back to Manchester Middle School!"

"Who says we're bringing you back?" said Liberty. "Seriously, I think she'd be fine as a colonist. I survived moving from one century to another and I think I'm a better horse because of it."

Elizabeth gasped, "You wouldn't dare!" She looked desperately at Tommy. "Thomas, you can't let them leave me here!"

Tommy looked at me and then back at Elizabeth. He finally said, "Elizabeth, you have a lot of things going for you, but nobody likes the way you treat them. You act like you're better than everyone else. You make Freedom feel like she's a fashion moron. You tell Liberty that he stinks. And you threaten to send Mr. Revere to a different school. And you want us to bring you back to Manchester Middle School so you can keep treating people like a piece of chewed gum stuck to the bottom of your shoe? No, thank you. If we bring you back, you're going to have to start treating people differently."

"Hey, I bring the teachers cupcakes!" Elizabeth said in defense.

"Only when you're trying to bribe them to give you a good grade," said Tommy. "Being truly nice to someone means being kind and thoughtful and considerate of others. It means complimenting Freedom about her hair or her smile or how smart she is."

"Okay, let's not go overboard," Elizabeth said.

"Being nice means not saying stuff that would make someone feel bad. For example, Liberty smells like a horse. He can't help it. It's just the way he is."

Elizabeth rolled her eyes. It was hard to know what she was thinking or feeling. She said, "Okay, I'm sorry, Liberty, for calling you odoriferous. But a body spray wouldn't hurt. Is that considered offensive?"

"Here's the thing, you'll know when you're really being nice when you do something for someone else without expecting anything in return."

"People actually do that?" Elizabeth gawked.

Suddenly, we heard the sound of a bell from a distant bell tower.

"You don't need to tell me what time it is!" Liberty grinned. "It starts with an *L* and ends with an *E*."

"Latrine?" asked Tommy. "Most people just say 'I have to go to the bathroom.'"

"Oh, brother," Liberty sighed. "It's lunchtime!"

The doors of Carpenters' Hall opened and several

George Washington, Patrick Henry, and Edmund Pendleton travel to the First Continental Congress at Carpenters' Hall, Philadelphia, September 1774.

distinguished-looking men dressed in colonial clothing exited the building. I didn't recognize most of them but some of them I did.

"Look, there's Patrick Henry!" Tommy said. "Can I go say hi?"

"Absolutely," I said.

"Come on, Elizabeth," Tommy said, "I'll introduce you. Cam is going to die when I tell him we bumped into Patrick Henry. He and Cam totally hit it off back in 1765."

Suddenly, I noticed Samuel Adams coming out of the building with two other men standing on either side of him. I didn't recognize the one on the left but the tall gentleman on the right was a dead ringer for George Washington!

"Liberty! Do you see who that is?" I pointed.

"Which one? Oh! I see. Wow! That's George Washington," Liberty whispered. "He's as regal as ever. I've always loved the way he commands respect. They should teach that in school."

"And exactly what would the class be called?" I asked, amused.

"Hmm," Liberty pondered, "how about *Awesomeness 101.* Seriously, George Washington is the man. People can't help but stare at him because he's just so awesome."

Within seconds, Samuel Adams, whom I had met in Boston, recognized me and said, "Rush Revere. Welcome! When did you arrive in Philadelphia?"

"Just today in fact," I said.

"Let me introduce you to my cousin John Adams, who is a fellow delegate from Massachusetts," said Samuel.

"A pleasure to meet you, sir," said John.

"You have no idea how excited I am to be here and meet all of you," I said, trembling with excitement. "I'm a history teacher and I've brought a couple of students with me."

A portrait of George Washington.

Portrait of John Adams by Gilbert Stuart.

"And what will you teach them about?" asked John Adams.

"Well, funny you should ask," I chuckled. "We are studying the events that led to the colonizing of America and the events leading up to the American Revolution."

"Yes, indeed, an American revolution. I like the sound of that," said the tall and regal-looking man who just had to be George Washington. "However, we must be united before we ever dare revolt. There is still much discord among the thirteen colonies."

Samuel Adams stepped forward and said, "Rush Revere, let me introduce you to one of our delegates from Virginia, the illustrious George Washington," said Samuel.

"I'm truly honored and overwhelmed," I said. "I barely know what to say. You are as presidential as I imagined."

"Are you running for political office, Mr. Washington?" asked John Adams.

"I doubt Mr. Washington is looking for this kind of office," I said knowingly.

"That is absolutely correct," said George Washington. "But I am looking for some food before we return to the Congress."

"Is George hungry again?" said a jovial voice from behind me. I turned to see Patrick Henry with Tommy and Elizabeth. Patrick laughed and slapped George Washington on the back. The future first president scowled and stood erect, ready to confront the man who dared invade his personal space. When he saw it was his fellow delegate Patrick Henry he only sighed, shook his head, and returned to his military posture.

Patrick laughed again and said, "I try to make sure that my fellow delegate from Virginia gets fed at least every other day but he seems to think he needs food every day!" This time everyone laughed, and even George Washington gave a half smile, but Patrick Henry laughed the loudest. "And where is my eloquent young friend, Cameron?" asked Patrick.

"I'm afraid he was unable to make this trip," I said. "But he is doing well and I know he will be sorry he missed you."

"It is good to be missed," said Patrick. "Better than being shot!" He laughed again and was joined by the others. "You must take this back to Cameron." Patrick raised his hand in the air and prompted me to do the same. When I did he slapped my upraised palm and said, "High five!" He laughed and exclaimed, "Cameron will know what that means."

I grinned and said, "Thank you, I'm sure he will enjoy it."

"And I am sure that my hunger grows more persistent," George Washington said. "Come, I know where we can get some hearty meat pies."

The others followed him as he led the way down a cobblestone street. His long stride and tall stature made him look the part of a natural leader.

"A good choice," said John Adams. "Meat pies are both delicious and filling. Even my cranky cousin would agree with me. Isn't that right, Samuel?"

"*Filling* is not the word I would choose," Samuel argued. "I prefer *satisfying*."

John rolled his eyes as the eight of us followed with growing appetites.

I marveled to think of who I was walking with. These were four of the Founding Fathers of America. And two of them, George Washington and John Adams, would be future presidents of the United States of America.

"Mr. Revere," Tommy said, "is Benjamin Franklin here?"

"No, he is not a delegate at this First Continental Congress," I said.

"I'm afraid he's licking his wounds after getting lambasted by Parliament for the Hutchinson letters," said John.

"The what letters?" asked Tommy.

John Adams continued: "The royal governor of Boston, Thomas Hutchinson, wrote letters to England asking for more British troops to fight against the American rebels as well as advice on how to subdue America by restricting its liberties. Somehow the letters were taken and printed in the Boston newspapers. As you can imagine, the citizens of Boston were furious and wanted Hutchinson's head. He had to flee to England and the British government demanded to know who leaked the letters."

"But what does that have to do with Benjamin Franklin?" asked Tommy.

John clarified, "At one point, Franklin had the letters in his possession. He was not responsible for the letters getting printed, but he took the blame so others who were innocent and wrongly accused would not get punished."

"He was verbally abused again and again. The brutal criticism must have been tormenting for him. It is said that he stood there silent yet standing firm. They wanted to show he was inferior and tried to make him feel worthless," said Samuel.

"The King and his Parliament think all the colonists in America are inferior. It is clear that they no longer consider us British citizens!" exclaimed Patrick Henry.

"I wish that were all that Franklin was dealing with," said George Washington. "It is well-known that Franklin's son,

Benjamin Franklin, assisted by his son William, proving the identity of electricity in lightning with his famous kite and key experiment of June, 1752.

Chaplain Jacob Duché leading the first prayer in the First Continental Congress at Carpenters' Hall, Philadelphia, September 1774.

William, is a fierce loyalist who refuses to listen to his father's pleas to join the Patriots. They have exchanged bitter words and I am sure it must feel as if he has lost his son to the darkness that blinds men of the truth."

"Indeed, it is a sad and difficult time for all who live in America," I said.

Tommy pulled me back with Liberty and Elizabeth and whispered, "I remember when we visited with Benjamin Franklin outside the Palace of Westminster. He was so kind and gave me some great fatherly advice."

Liberty butted in and whispered, "He called you the Future of America, remember?"

"Yeah." Tommy nodded. "How can his son not see and appreciate a father with so much wisdom and goodness? But I suppose we don't really know what happens inside of families."

Liberty nodded and whispered, "Remember when Benjamin called me a *natural phenomenon*? And he said I was exactly who I was meant to be. He basically said I was awesome and the most amazing creature on the planet."

"Are you sure he didn't say you're naturally delusional and the most annoying creature on the planet?" asked Elizabeth with an attitude.

"Ahh, there's the Elizabeth we all know and love." I smiled. "It's good to have you join in the conversation."

Elizabeth just rolled her eyes and turned the other way.

"Here! We have arrived at our destination," said George Washington.

Before too long I was eating a slice of warm meat pie made with ground pork, potatoes, onions, and spices. It was absolutely delicious.

"I'm going to that vegetable cart," whispered Elizabeth. "I'm not a big fan of meat pies."

"I'm coming with you," whispered Liberty. "I'm not a carnivore."

I called to Tommy and said, "Why don't you go with Elizabeth and Liberty."

Elizabeth gave me a suspicious look and said, "What? You think I'm going to escape with Liberty when you're not looking?"

"It's not that I don't trust you, Elizabeth," I said. "Oh, wait, on second thought, I don't trust you." I smiled.

"Whatever," she said as she headed toward the vegetable cart.

I turned to these legendary Founding Fathers and asked, "I know you are about to make a decision that could separate America from Great Britain. Are you truly ready to face the consequences of this decision? I'm sure you know that King George will not give up without a fight."

Patrick Henry squared his shoulders to mine and boldly said, "As God is my witness I say give me liberty or give me death. I will give my life for the cause of freedom. I will not support a crown that restricts our liberties. I will not pay the King's debt or feed his soldiers or obey without question. He will take everything from us if we let him. Parliament laughs at the thought of us governing ourselves. It is time we make America free!"

"But we are a free people," said John Adams. "Always were and always will be. As the first colonists arrived on the *Mayflower* and fought the elements, we will fight against tyranny always!"

"We may be hanged, but we will die for our beloved freedom!" Samuel Adams joined in.

I nodded as George Washington stepped forward. As he spoke it was as if the clouds parted and the sun rested upon

his back and shoulders. He smiled as he looked down at each of us before saying, "America was founded on freedom. Heaven opened a way for the Puritans to come and thrive in a hard and hostile land. Were they smart men? Of course they were. But I have read that men like William Bradford were more than just smart. They were people of faith and courage and integrity. I believe the only way America can prosper is to remember the religious freedoms that our forefathers fought for. Only then can the smiles of heaven bless this sacred land."

We all nodded at the wisdom from the man who would be the first president of the greatest nation on earth. And for a quick moment I thought of my Pilgrim hero William Bradford and how sad he would be to hear that all the freedoms that they fled England for were in jeopardy. But how happy he would be to know that many brave men in this century were fighting to keep their dreams alive!

"This Congress," I said. "Do you think it has been successful?"

"This First Continental Congress represents the willingness of the thirteen separate colonies to join together as one united government," said Patrick.

"Sort of like a united states of America?" I hinted.

"Yes, you could say that," said John Adams. "In fact, I quite like the thought of it."

"And now we must return to vote as a united America," John said.

"We must all pray more fervently that God will help us in this most important decision," said Patrick Henry.

Tommy, Elizabeth, Liberty, and I were outside Carpenters' Hall when the final session of the First Continental Congress ended. I'll admit I was extremely anxious to know if the colonies decided to separate from England or not. As the doors opened and the delegates began exiting the building I saw Samuel Adams first.

"I'll be right back," I said as I ran to learn the real history of what had happened.

Samuel looked satisfied as he said, "A vote was taken and the delegates of the First Continental Congress decided to cut off colonial trade with Great Britain unless Parliament abolishes the Intolerable Acts."

"If I'm not mistaken," I mused, "the Intolerable Acts caused the port of Boston to be closed, forced the people of Boston to open their homes so the King's soldiers would have a place to live, and denied any Bostonian to govern their own city."

"That is correct," said Samuel. "The King must reopen Boston Harbor, remove the Redcoats from living in our homes, allow Boston to govern itself, and remove other punitive laws."

"And you are happy with this?" I asked.

"Yes, of course," Samuel said. "But the delegates were asked to return to their colonies and begin training their citizens for potential war against Britain."

A sense of worry and dread touched my heart and mind. My own feelings surprised me. I knew the history. I knew the outcome. So why did I feel so much angst about the news from Samuel? As I pondered I realized what it was. Simply, war means death. The men, women, and children that I had seen in Massachusetts and Virginia, the families in all the colonies, would sacrifice so much for something many Americans today take for granted. Freedom. Is freedom something worth dying for? I believe it is. But not all the delegates were happy about this. However, in the end the votes were cast and the decision was made to officially make a stand against the King of England.

And I knew that in less than six months the war for America's independence would officially begin at the Battle of Lexington.

"Godspeed, Rush Revere," said Samuel.

"Godspeed, Samuel Adams," I said in return.

As I walked back toward my little band of time travelers I noticed that Tommy, Elizabeth, and Liberty had walked over to a group of boys about thirty yards away. It looked like they were taunting and teasing Elizabeth and, no surprise, Elizabeth wasn't standing for it.

As I got closer I began to hear their conversation.

"You don't belong in America!" said a large colonial boy.

"I was born in America, you idiots!" shouted Elizabeth. "You all stink like pigs. It's like you haven't bathed in days!"

The boys thought that was the funniest thing ever. "We do not bathe," they all said.

"But we think you should jump in the sea and swim back to your precious England," said a boy with red hair.

"Hey, maybe we should send her back with a little gift for the King," laughed a scrawny kid who was missing a front tooth and carrying a wooden bucket.

The other boys cheered him on and before I could interfere, the scrawny kid ran up to Elizabeth with the wooden bucket. My fears were realized when I saw a mess of soupy mud launch from the bucket with deadly aim toward Elizabeth's face and dress. Suddenly, everything stopped and everything was silent. The mud hung in the air like an ugly piece of modern art. The boys pointed and laughed like they were colonial statues. I looked for Liberty, certain he was behind this. Unblinking, Liberty's eyes were focused like lasers on Elizabeth. Although everything in the past had ceased moving, those of us from the future were still free to act. In a flash, Tommy quickly moved Elizabeth several feet to the left and that's when Liberty finally blinked and everything went back to normal.

The mud splashed to the ground and the boy with the bucket looked shocked that he had missed his target by that much. His friends laughed at the scrawny kid like he was the one that got covered in mud.

Elizabeth was stunned and confused at the same time. "What just . . . how did . . ."

"It was Liberty," said Tommy. "He can do more than just open a portal to the past."

As we walked away from the boys, Liberty stood between Elizabeth and the menacing boys like he was protecting her.

"Why did you do that?" Elizabeth asked Liberty. "Why did you help me when I've been so mean to you?"

"Maybe we aren't friends yet," Liberty said. "But we could be. And I wanted to show you that I don't hold any grudges. America is a land of the free where people, like the Pilgrims and the colonists, were able to start over in a new place with a new life."

"True, but it's not free of bullies," said Tommy.

"No," said Liberty, "unfortunately, there will always be bullies. But that's why friends are so important."

"That's right," I said. "When the colonists in Boston were bullied by King George and his Intolerable Acts, twelve other colonies were willing to help and support their sister colony."

"We're sort of like secret sisters now," Liberty chuckled. "Well, except I'm a male and we don't have the same mother and if we did that would be really weird."

"This whole thing is weird!" said Elizabeth firmly. "I-I think I just want to go back to the school now."

"I think that's a good idea," I said.

Within minutes we found a secluded place to time-jump. Within seconds we were back at Manchester Middle School. Elizabeth quickly dismounted and ran off like Cinderella at midnight.

"That was weird," said Tommy.

"Maybe she had to go to the bathroom," Liberty said.

"I think Elizabeth is at a crossroads right now," I said. "I believe her greed for power and her need for friendship are battling inside of her."

"Well, I hope the good Elizabeth wins," said Liberty. "The evil one scares me."

"Thanks, again, Mr. Revere," said Tommy. "And thanks, Liberty. It's been another amazing adventure through time."

"I'm glad you enjoyed it," I said. "And I almost forgot, you better take these with you." I pulled out the three musket balls from my coat pocket. As I did, I purposefully let a small seed packet slip from my pocket and land in front of Tommy's feet.

"You dropped something," Tommy said.

"Oh, clumsy me," I said. "I'd only meant to give you these musket balls for good luck. They seemed to help you with your last game so I thought you might enjoy having these before your next one."

"Oh, yeah, I forgot about those. Thanks!" said Tommy. He eyed the small packet I had in my other hand and asked, "So what's with the little packet? Hey, does that say 'From B. Franklin' on it?"

"Oh, this?" I said, innocently. "Yes, well, these are from Benjamin Franklin. I'd forgotten he gave these to me the last time we visited. It's an experiment he's been working on and he said he finally succeeded in creating the first spaghetti seeds."

"Spaghetti seeds?" Tommy asked.

"Yes," I replied, "apparently these seeds can grow spaghetti noodles in your garden."

"That's amazing!" Tommy said. "That guy can do anything! Any chance I could try them in my mom's garden?"

"I don't see why not. Just take these and bring me back what you don't use," I said, handing Tommy the packet.

"Awesome, thanks! See ya!" he said as he jogged up the stairs and into the school.

As I watched Tommy leave, Liberty said, "When do you think he'll discover that those spaghetti seeds are fake? Personally, I'm surprised he fell for it."

"Me, too," I chuckled. "Let's go and get some breakfast. How about bagels and cream cheese?"

"Sounds good to me!"

As we started to leave the school, I was surprised to see Elizabeth again. She had already changed into her modern-day clothes and was waiting for us by the big oak tree. As we got closer she quickly handed me a small disk.

"What's this?" I asked.

"Just take it before I change my mind," Elizabeth abruptly replied.

I reached out and took the disk.

"It's the memory card from my video camera," Elizabeth said.

"The blackmail video?" Liberty asked.

Elizabeth sighed. "It sounds so mean when you say it like that. But, yes, it's the video of you and Mr. Revere jumping through the time portal."

"Thank you, Elizabeth," I said, sincerely.

"Yes, thank you," said Liberty. "What happened? I mean I don't know if you realize this or not but what you're doing right now could be considered, um, well, it could be considered a *nice gesture."*

"Whatever," Elizabeth said as she looked around to see if anyone was watching.

"Seriously," Liberty continued. "If word got out that you were doing nice things for other people, well, your reputation could be ruined."

Elizabeth kept her head down and her arms folded. I could tell she was trying to decide what to say next. Finally, she lifted her head and looked at Liberty. Her voice cracked just a little when she said, "You protected me. You know, back in Philadelphia. So I . . . I wanted to thank you. You helped me and now I'm helping you. Now we're even." As she turned to leave she looked one last time at me and said, "Mr. Revere, just to be clear, you and I are *not* even. I believe it was your plan to throw me into that pond at Windsor castle. Anyway, you haven't seen the last of me. And I can't wait until our next adventure," she said with a smirk. With a flip of her long blond hair she turned and walked away.

"Don't you just love happy endings," said Liberty, smiling.

Happy endings? "Maybe for you," I mumbled and decided that maybe I should start sleeping with one eye open.

As we walked away from Manchester Middle School, Liberty asked, "Who did you enjoy visiting the most? Benjamin Franklin? Patrick Henry? Samuel Adams? Paul Revere . . ."

I laughed and said, "Well, they were all very different. Benjamin Franklin's creative energy, his calm wisdom, and his brilliant mind were certainly gifts to America. His speech in Parliament may have been the reason that the King finally repealed the

Stamp Act. And I know he plays a bigger role in the Second Continental Congress and the Declaration of Independence."

"And . . ." Liberty prodded.

"And Patrick Henry's bold and courageous speeches against the King's injustice created a spark for the American Revolution. I loved his enthusiasm for life and his courage to defend freedom. Oh, and I must remember to give Cam his high five from Patrick Henry."

"And did you ever warm up to the Samuelator?" Liberty joked.

"Are you kidding? I loved Samuel Adams! I mean he wasn't really looking for friends, he was looking for freedom and he never doubted the cause."

"Well, he always seemed a little angry to me," Liberty said.

"Some people call it anger. I call it one hundred percent colonial stubbornness! It was a determination mixed with a whole lot of passion. He was always ready to tell people what to believe. He was a fire starter and really good at fanning the flames of the Revolution!"

"And, of course, your boyhood hero, Paul Revere!" Liberty said with a big smile.

"Wow, he was involved in everything," I said. "He was ready to serve wherever he was needed. He was strong, talented, happy, I mean, what's not to like! He's the kind of guy I want as my next-door neighbor. Dependable, always there when you need him. And his courage as a Patriot with the Sons of Liberty is exactly what America needed. Although, I plan to see more of him. I mean we definitely need to time-jump to witness his famous midnight ride!"

"Oooh, I'm all for that!" Liberty nodded.

"What about you?" I asked. "Who impressed you the most?"

"Not who, but what!" Liberty said. "For me it was all about freedom."

"What's all about me?" asked Freedom, who surprised me from behind.

"You startled me," I said.

"I knew you were there," said Liberty. "I could sense you a mile away!"

"I'm glad you're back," said Freedom. "So, what about me?" she asked again as she slung her backpack to her other shoulder. "Liberty said something like it was all about Freedom."

"Not you," Liberty corrected. "It's all about fighting for freedom. That's what I've learned the most the last few days."

"Me, too," Freedom said. "I mean I haven't always believed that. But I think Samuel Adams is right when he said my freedom is worth fighting for. Sometimes we really do have to fight to live free. So starting today I'm going to start living my name! You're looking at the new Freedom!"

"Good for you!" I said.

"Yeah," Liberty agreed. "You look different already!"

"Speaking of looking different," said Freedom suspiciously as she reached out for the Indian feathers still in Liberty's mane. "What are these? Oh, that's right. You guys visited the Boston Tea Party! That was so weird that we could talk to each other through time."

"I know, right?" said Liberty.

"Well, I better get to my first class," said Freedom, laughing, as she skipped toward the school. "But tell me all about your trip on my way to school. You know, telepathically! Oh, and bye,

Mr. Revere! Great seeing you! Did I mention that having free-dom is a great feeling!" she yelled, skipping backward. "And it's worth fighting for!"

"Well, that was fun!" said Liberty. "For the record, I think your students really like you as their substitute history teacher, especially Freedom, Tommy, and Cam. Oh, and we never got to tell Cam about our adventure at the First Continental Con-gress! Maybe I'll meet him for lunch and give him all the details. Hmm, I know it's still early, but lunch sounds really good about now." Instantly, Liberty looked panicked and said, "Wait a min-ute, have we eaten breakfast? With all the excitement I almost skipped a meal!"

The excitement has just begun, I thought as I patted Liberty. America was definitely feeling growing pains. It was plagued with evils like slavery and burdened by a tyrant king. It was clear our country was not perfect and neither were our Founding Fathers. But our visit with these exceptional Americans had re-minded me what it means to fight for freedom and endure hard things. More than ever I was ready for our next adventure and the truths we would learn about the American Revolution!

Be sure to explore the *Adventures of Rush Revere* at
www.twoifbytea.com!

David and Rush

Acknowledgments

There isn't a single day when I don't sincerely appreciate my loyal, unwavering audience, great people who make me eager to wake up each day and join them on the radio. The bond of loyalty that has developed over the past twenty-five years still has me in awe and I am more motivated than ever each day to meet and surpass their expectations. You really have no idea how much I appreciate and love you all. My heartfelt appreciation further extends to all of the children, parents, grandparents, aunts, and uncles across America who love this phenomenal country like I do. Their support over the years has allowed me to want to take on new projects like this one because I know we are unified in our mission to teach the younger generations why the United States is a place to be cherished.

Once again I give thanks and have tremendous gratitude to my wife, Kathryn, for developing and shepherding this series. She manages and coordinates all aspects of the assembly of the many parts that make up each book. She is tireless and devoted beyond a level I deserve. Her intelligent creativity and insight are unparalleled. I am indeed a lucky man.

ACKNOWLEDGMENTS

Writing a book for children is brand-new for me and I could not do it without our incredible small team pouring their very hearts into every aspect of the undertaking. It requires countless hours going over every detail. Nothing is farmed out, nothing is phoned in. There are no half measures taken. Their commitment and passion make this something special to be part of. Thank you to Christopher Schoebinger for your creativity, adaptability, and devotion from day one. You are the Best. Thank you to Chris Hiers for the unbelievable attention to detail and perfection in every illustration. Spero Mehallis defines loyal and hardworking.

Jonathan Adams Rogers has been indispensable. There aren't many about whom that can be said. I sincerely appreciate his dedication and help, which was limitless while also being great.

My brother, David Limbaugh, grants us all peace of mind. His unwavering support of every endeavor and positive attitude is a constant inspiration.

After hearing about the idea to create a children's series, my good friend, the late Vince Flynn, put me in touch with Louise Burke at Simon & Schuster. Thank you to Vince, Louise, and everyone at Simon & Schuster, especially Mitchell Ivers, who helped bring this vision to life.

Photo Credits

65	Chris Hiers
70	Peter Tillemans, Getty Images
73	Chris Hiers
78	Image Asset Management Ltd./SuperStock
85	Chris Hiers
95	Chris Hiers
97	SuperStock
105	Chris Hiers
109	Chris Hiers
116	Chris Hiers
119	© The Print Collector/Corbis
122	National Portrait Gallery/SuperStock
129	Chris Hiers
131	Prism/Superstock
136	Chris Hiers
142	The Granger Collection, NYC
144	The Granger Collection, NYC
147	Library of Congress
148	Wikimedia Commons
151	Getty Images
161	Getty Images
165	The Granger Collection, NYC
169	Everett Collection/SuperStock
173	The Granger Collection, NYC
175	Chris Hiers
177	Images Etc Ltd., Getty Images
183	Wikimedia Commons
186	Getty Images
190	Chris Hiers
203	Chris Hiers
208	The Granger Collection, NYC
210	Superstock
211	National Gallery of Art
215	SuperStock
216	The Granger Collection, NYC
219	Chris Hiers

PHOTO CREDITS

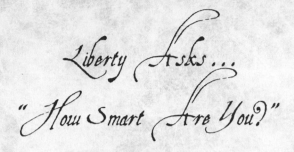

Liberty Asks . . .

"How Smart Are You?"

(Beware—He Thinks He Can Stump You!)

1. What kind of animal is the Manchester Middle School mascot?
2. How many colonies were there in 1774?
3. What is the prank that Tommy and Cam played in front of the class?
4. Who invented swim fins?
5. What is Liberty's favorite type of food in Boston?
6. In what city can the Palace of Westminster be found?
7. What were the British soldiers called?
8. Who played the fiddle in the tavern?
9. True or false, the Stamp Act meant that no one could use postage stamps on their envelopes?
10. In what country can Windsor Castle be found?
11. In what city did the famous massacre take place described in this book?
12. Which patriot is Rush Revere's idol?

13. Who identified that there is electricity in lightning?

14. Who lived at Windsor Castle?

15. True or false: the Quartering Act of 1765 required the colonists to house British soldiers?

16. What did members of the crowd shout at Patrick Henry when he spoke in the Virginia House of Burgesses?

17. What was Paul Revere's profession?

18. What did they throw off the boats in Boston Harbor?

19. What famous American spoke in front of British Parliament about the Stamp Act?

20. What is the meeting that Rush Revere, Ben Franklin, George Washington, and others attended at the end of the book called?

Looking for answers?

Visit the *Adventures of Rush Revere* at www.twoifbytea.com!

Do you know what this is?

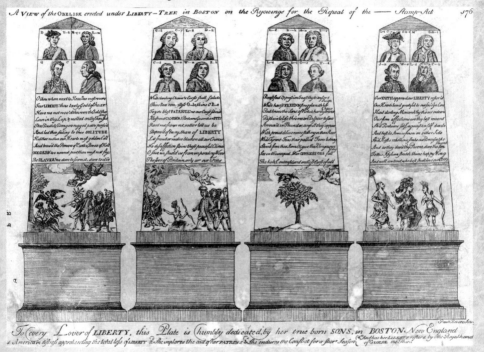

An obelisk engraved by Paul Revere and erected under Liberty Tree
in Boston to celebrate the repeal of the Stamp Act, 1766.